ON
THIS
ROCKNE

ALSO BY RALPH MCINERNY,
IN HIS FATHER DOWLING
MYSTERY SERIES:

Her Death of Cold
The Seventh Station
Bishop as Pawn
Lying Three
Second Vespers
Thicker Than Water
A Loss of Patients
The Grass Widow
Getting a Way with Murder
Rest in Pieces
The Basket Case
Abracadaver
Four on the Floor
Judas Priest
Desert Sinner
Seed of Doubt
A Cardinal Offense
The Tears of Things

ON THIS ROCKNE

A Notre Dame Mystery

RALPH McINERNY

DOUBLEDAY DIRECT LARGE PRINT EDITION

St. Martin's Press   New York

This Large Print Edition, prepared especially for Doubleday Direct, Inc., contains the complete unabridged text of the original Publisher's Edition.

ISBN 1-56865-523-1

**This Large Print Book carries the
Seal of Approval of N.A.V.H.**

TO ARNOLD MCINERNY

Member of the Notre Dame football team.

Killed in action at Château-Thierry, July 1918.

A man whose loyalty to his school, to his friends and his country, whose gentlemanly conduct, scholarly attitude, courage and conviction, and high sense of honor make him an ideal of which Notre Dame is justly proud.

ON
THIS
ROCKNE

When Marcus Bramble '57 decided to give the University of Notre Dame the wherewithal to raise a fitting monument to its legendary coach, Knute Rockne, he announced it to the world. The university administration first heard of it in the way everybody else did, via the national news.

"Rockne is among the half dozen most important figures in American sports," Bramble said, looking up at the interviewer. Bramble owned an NBA team as well as an NHL team and he was an often-photographed figure, dwarfed by his millionaire employees.

The reporter wondered if Notre Dame hadn't already honored its coach.

"The Rockne Memorial?" Bramble laughed a cheerless laugh. "The only thing it had was a swimming pool and that's obsolete."

"What are you proposing?"

Bramble looked sly. "Something big. Big." He rose on tiptoe as he said it.

"A new stadium?"

An enigmatic smile. "Let me ask you a question. Where's Rockne buried?"

"I don't know."

"See?"

"Kansas? Some place in Kansas."

The interview ended on Bramble's mocking laughter.

The sum mentioned was ten million dollars which, even with inflation and affluence, was not a negligible contribution to the university. Understandably, the subject was much discussed on campus.

"He's in the community cemetery, isn't he?" Professor Ward asked, and silence fell as the others at the Old Bastards table in the University Club stared at him.

"Rockne in the community cemetery?"

Professor Brady managed a nice meld of wonder and contempt as he repeated this.

Ward was informed that there were only two lay people buried in the little cemetery reserved for deceased members of the Congregation of the Holy Cross which was located on the road to St. Mary's, where the road to Moreau Seminary cuts off.

"Who are they?"

"Father Zahm's brother is one, the NASA guy."

"Who else?"

"Frank O'Malley."

"Don't forget Father John A. O'Brien. He's over there and he's no CSC."

"But he was a priest. Anyway, he bought his way in."

"To a cemetery?"

John A. O'Brien had been a pamphleteer and editor of a series of books on converts to the faith. He had been in residence at Notre Dame during the last years of his life, a short man with an upper body that bent forward and a wisp of wavy white hair on an oversized head. A legendary ascetic, he had worn a cassock that was green with age.

"And he golfed with wooden-shafted

clubs," Brady noted. You could count on Brady for the significant, sometimes accurate, detail.

It may not have been true that O'Brien subsisted on bread and water, but he had been notoriously parsimonious. In his will, written with pencil on a sheet of lined paper, he left everything he possessed, otherwise unspecified, to Notre Dame. This turned out to be millions. It went to endow half a dozen professorial chairs.

"You think Bramble wants to put Rockne in there with the priests?"

"A ten-million-dollar grave? Come on."

"What else could it be?"

Brady suggested a pyramid on the main quad. Ward wondered if there wasn't room under one of those relic altars in Sacred Heart Basilica.

"Wasn't Rockne a convert?"

"I wonder if there is anyone still alive who actually knew him."

"You could check Holy Cross House."

"I was just wondering."

At the jock table, which was closer to the bar, Jim Carberry was leading a seminar on club rules. Smoking was still permitted at lunch, but was now prohibited in the evening. The venerable chemical engineer had earned a seat at the athletic table because of a stint few now remembered coaching interhall football.

"I thought you quit smoking."

"That's right, *I* did. But no one quit for me. This is fascism."

Hank Fraily sent a thin stream of cigar smoke toward the center of the table where it first blossomed and then dissipated. Father Riehle responded in kind, then asked, "What would be a fitting Rockne memorial?"

"A remake of the movie?"

"He's only giving ten million dollars."

Elsewhere others were pained by this reminder of the original basis of the university's national fame. Conspicuous signs at campus entrances now announced that Notre Dame was a National Catholic Research University. Throughout the Hesburgh years, great efforts had been made at least to match on the academic side the athletic reputation of Notre Dame, and great progress had been made. But schizophrenia persisted. For alumni, real and

subway, it was football that united them to
the school that had been raised on the Indiana prairie in the mid-nineteenth century
and had risen to prominence during its
more than century and a half of existence.

"Hesburgh should have gotten rid of football."

"Like Hutchins."

A sigh. The University of Chicago was an
acceptable measure of what a university
ought to be.

"Didn't they have a legendary coach
too?"

"Amos Alonzo Stagg."

"And they lived it down."

"The same thing could have happened
here. There was a narrow window of opportunity in the early fifties."

These were not professors who would recall with pain names like Terry Brennan
and Joe Kuharich, coaches whose careers
had marked the pre-Faust nadir of Notre
Dame football, but they knew, or thought
they knew, that Father Ted had toyed with
the idea of dropping football.

"We could have joined the Ivy League."

Sighs in the committee room.

In the administration building, the president had finally reached Marcus Bramble by telephone.

"You've given us quite a surprise, Marcus." The priest was a decade younger than the alumnus, but his tone was avuncular.

"It's all true, Father."

"It would be nice if you could fly out for an official announcement."

"Oh, it's official. I told Father Ted."

The president directed a pained smile at those sitting around his desk. He was in his third term in office yet many persisted in thinking that his predecessor was still at the helm. Father Hesburgh, in his aerie on the thirteenth floor of the library named for him, had kept ostentatiously out of the way of his successors, but for many, Father Ted was still the real president. Historic building binges had failed to etch the name of the later presidents on the minds and imaginations of those concerned with Notre Dame, let alone of the great public beyond.

"Did you ask him to tell me?"

"Hey, Father, it's no secret."

The president offered to fly to Denver to

accept the benefaction, but Bramble said he would be in South Bend for the first home game.

"You will be my guest, Marcus."

When he hung up, his expression was not that of the beneficiary of a wealthy and generous alumnus. The generosity was not to be despised, but it must be diverted to an institutionally acceptable purpose.

"Where is Rockne buried?"

"I'll look it up."

2

When Roger Knight was asked to join the Notre Dame faculty, his reaction had been mixed. On the one hand, it was an opportunity to live the life he had been ostensibly preparing himself for when he earned his Princeton Ph.D. years before. On the other hand, no small amount of time had elapsed since he was nineteen and newly *doctoratus*. At the time, he had been too young to expect a regular academic appointment and, though of course no one mentioned this, he was far too fat as well. On a romantic impulse he had decided to join the Navy, which was not at all reluctant to draw attention to his avoir-dupois. He lost nearly a hundred pounds in order to pass the physical, but not so much that he did not float through the mandatory swimming test. After boot camp, most memories of which he had suppressed, he spent two enjoyable years reading through the base libraries at several stateside postings. He had never been at sea. Or, a hostile interpretation, he had always been metaphorically at sea and wouldn't have known the literal difference. When he got out of the navy, he lived with his older brother Philip, a private detective, putting his electronic skills at Philip's service. At the time of the Notre Dame overture, they were living in Rye, New York, and it was there that he spoke with the envoy from Notre Dame.

"I'm emeritus myself," Father Carmody said, "but Emil Huneker was an old friend. The family is counting on me to make sure that the occupant of the Huneker Chair is someone extraordinary."

"I guess I qualify there." Roger was no longer at naval tonnage but his present weight was double what it had been in graduate school.

"Your book on Baron Corvo was a tour de force."

It had also been, to everyone's amazement, a commercial success. Baron Corvo, Frederick Rolfe, was a half-mad turn-of-the-century convert whose desire to become a priest had been thwarted and who then wrote a number of vindictive and relentlessly autobiographical novels that had always had their devotees. Roger's book had occasioned their reprinting. There was also renewed interest in the other figures Roger had mentioned.

"Who thinks of Ronald Firbank as Catholic?" Father Carmody asked.

"Don't forget Oscar Wilde."

The priest winced. "Didn't he die repentant?"

"Let us hope so."

The Huneker Chair was meant to bring back to Notre Dame the approach to literature associated with the legendary Frank O'Malley. O'Malley had taught courses in such Catholic novelists as Mauriac, Bernanos, Greene, and Waugh.

"My degree is in philosophy, Father."

"Frank also taught a course in the philosophy of Catholic literature. Your book is in literature."

"What would the department think?"

"Probably what they thought of Frank. It doesn't matter. This is a university chair. You will be a department unto yourself."

After leaving Princeton, Roger had surprised himself by not missing the academic world. The navy was an anodyne. Later, he did not think of the scholars with whom he came to communicate by the Internet as mere academics. One e-mail friend was Professor of Hittite at the University of Chicago, at work on a dictionary of that language which intrigued Roger, but mostly they exchanged messages on baseball. The joys of such exchanges were a far cry from teaching. A teacher must first find where his students are and start from there. Roger had never quite believed that the beginning points were as far back as they apparently were.

"It would be quite a change, Father Carmody."

"You would be a tremendous addition to the faculty."

"Literally, perhaps. Do you happen to

know how many novels Knute Rockne wrote?"

Father Carmody looked warily at Roger. "Why do you think he wrote any?"

"Because I have one of them. *The Four Winners.*"

"I don't know it."

Roger took it as a joke and Father Carmody got them back on the important thing.

"You were the first one I thought of when the Huneker Chair was established."

"It has never been occupied?"

"You will be the first."

At least he would not be measured by another's standards. "Wouldn't it be wiser if I came as a visitor first?"

Father Carmody didn't like that. But that in the end was the arrangement. Temporary lodging was provided on campus, with plenty of room for Philip as well.

"What exactly does your brother do?"

"He is a private detective."

"His office is in Rye?"

"In a manner of speaking."

Philip had departed Manhattan after a second mugging convinced him that the city was no longer habitable. But he continued in his profession by advertising in the Yellow Pages of half a dozen major cities, giving an 800 number but no indication of where Philip Knight and Associate were located. Roger was the associate, but there seemed no need to tell Father Carmody that Dr. Roger Knight was also a licensed private detective. Philip took only such jobs as interested him and then retreated to the idyllic setting of Rye for a restorative interlude.

"South Bend or Rye," Philip said when Roger asked him how the move would affect him. "What's the difference?"

"Well, I suppose we could try it and see."

"Notre Dame," Philip said reverently. Of course he was thinking of football. Roger was thinking of the library with its special collections and of the university's long tradition stretching back to 1842. His loyalty to the church he had joined while a student at Princeton was fervent and unquestioning, and Notre Dame was of course the most visible symbol of the faith in the United States. There were one or two things other than football taking place on the South Bend campus.

They moved to South Bend, they were

established in an apartment in the Hesburgh International Center, conveniently
close to the University Club and the Morris
Inn but some distance from the Hesburgh
Library, where Roger spent much of his day
and where he offered his seminar in Paul
Claudel. Phil spent happy morning hours in
the Loftus Center, exercising and chatting
with Lefty Smith about Notre Dame athletics and in the afternoon watched football
practice. Roger was at his computer, answering e-mail, when Phil brought home
the news of the Bramble donation.

"What kind of a memorial?"

"Everyone's asking that same question."

3

The question continued to be asked during the week and a half before the first home game. From a distance, enigmatic remarks from the donor increased the speculation. Bramble was regularly interviewed after his NFL team played and inevitably now brought the discussion around to his alma mater and his intention to honor Knute Rockne. What did Mr. Bramble have in mind? He all but leered into the camera in response to this and brought a finger to his lips. In the main building, an ad hoc committee attempted to gain control of the situation, but they were advancing across a minefield. Getting the ten million dollars without strings and restrictions was the aim. How to achieve that aim was far from clear.

"We mustn't seem to be putting down Rockne," a vice-president warned.

Heads around the table nodded. None there had known Rockne. None there had even known Leahy. Few could so much as remember the era of Ara Parseghian. And there were those among them who were less than enthusiastic about the triumphs of Lou Holtz. Behind these ambiguous reactions lurked a nagging question, never quite articulated. Was a top-ten team compatible with a national research university?

"Bramble keeps referring to Rockne's grave."

"He wants to bury him on campus."

"Where?"

"He mentioned Orestes Brownson."

"My God."

Beneath a stone in the main aisle of the basement church lay the remains of Orestes Brownson, the great nineteenth-century religious controversialist whose stormy spiritual aeneid had ended in the Catholic Church and whose body came to rest beneath the floor of the lower church on the campus of Notre Dame. Over the years, the feet of worshipers had worn the stone smooth, all but erasing its Latin legend. Did Bramble imagine a similar resting place in the upper church for Knute Rockne?

"We have to come up with an alternative."

"To praise Rockne, not to bury him?" The faculty representative smirked as he said it, but the allusion was not recognized.

No viable alternative occurred to the committee, but they were agreed they would not rebury Knute Rockne on campus. What the university did not want at this point in its history was the suggestion that its heart and soul were to be found in its phenomenally successful athletic programs.

A resolution was introduced in the academic senate demanding that the faculty be consulted on the matter of the Bramble benefaction. The discussion made it clear that it was not the particular donation alone that interested the senate. The resolution was part of a concerted effort to implement the idea of self-governance to which the administration gave lip service. To be fair, no administrator had ever thought of the faculty senate, notoriously a safety valve where professors whose careers had not gone well could make speeches to one another, as playing any part in the governance of the university.

Senator Xanthippe Fondus, a stocky redhead from theology, expressed her shock that the senate should bother itself with such matters. It was one thing for there to be a gap between the administration's rhetoric and its practice, but she trusted that the senate took seriously this institution's intention to evolve into a first-rate university.

"You mean a spot in the sportswriters' top ten?"

"I do not understand the reference."

"There's a research project for you."

This exchange was with Casey Basquette, a surly veteran of thirty-seven years on the faculty and twenty on the senate who could be counted on to take the opposite on any question. He had been the occasion of the one certified *mot* on the part of the senate president who once, when Basquette was in full flight, had remarked, "Our gadfly is open."

"There is a motion on the table," someone shouted.

"We are discussing it."

"Vote, vote."

The discussion soon descended into the
labyrinthine intricacies of parliamentary
procedure from which it was unlikely to
emerge for hours.

In the Corby Hall dining room, the residence for CSC priests who were not
assigned to student residences, the congregation congregated at tables according
to generation, an informal arrangement,
having only the sanction of tradition. Those
whose service antedated Vatican II were a
dwindling band at a table near the kitchen
doors through which waitresses came and
went. Father Carmody had passed on to
his fellow religious Roger Knight's remark
about Rockne's novel and the topic came
up at intervals at the preconciliar table.

"We don't have a copy here," "Candy"
Whitman said, concealing his mouth with
his napkin.

"Sure we do."

"I just looked."

"What's wrong with your mouth?"

"I've been to the dentist."

"Ah." The bowl of oatmeal before Whitman was thus explained. "Did you check the books in your room?"

"It is not in my room."

"I have a copy," Anthony Smith said.

The topic was *The Four Winners*. Smith had taught English and was now emeritus. His offer to give a course or two had not been taken up by the English Department but, as he confessed, he didn't know a soul in the department anymore.

"Is the copy your own?"

"I *own* nothing," Smith said prissily. They all had taken the three vows of religion, Poverty, Obedience, and Chastity. At this table it would be remembered that once they had written in their breviaries and other books, *ad usum Patris Smith* or whatever.

"What's it like?"

"Pretty bad. Like Rockne himself, I wouldn't dig it up again."

"I like it," Ned Joyce said. "It's got drive. It tells a story."

"What's the name of the university in the novel?"

"Dulac."

Mild laughter. "That would really throw the reader off."

"It's about Notre Dame?"

"It's about football. Not much else happens at Dulac."

"No wonder those people are furious with Bramble." "Those people" was the table's term of art for the current administration of the university.

"What do you think he wants done, Ned?"

But Father Ned Joyce, having laid down the burdens of office had driven all such thoughts from his mind. Let those people worry about Bramble and his money. He moved his hands in a gesture of indifference.

"You should care. You already have your monument."

The Joyce Athletic and Convocation Center, two huge geodesic domes linked by a central area that housed the display of the university's athletic history, was named for Joyce, who had been Father Hesburgh's right-hand man for decades.

"Is there room for a tomb over there, Ned?"

Smith's oatmeal was taken away and he was given tea and toast. He looked with envy at the plates of the others.

"Don't drool," he was advised. "Tomorrow you will be an indentured servant like the rest of us."

4

After the second meeting of his seminar on the drama of Paul Claudel, Roger was asked by a student, Katherine George, if he would direct her dissertation. Roger was taken aback.

"Are you in English?"

"No. Modern languages."

"How much course work have you done?"

"This is my first semester as a graduate student."

Roger relaxed. Katherine was a lovely girl with almond eyes, dark hair, and a perpetual expression of puzzled wonderment. Her dissertation was years in the future, so her surprising request posed no immediate problem.

"Where did you do your undergraduate work?"

"Here."

"What was your major?"

"Preprofessional." She waited for his re-action. "I changed my mind. I began to read Ionescu."

"Ionescu!"

"My French is very good." She said this matter-of-factly.

"Have you read Claudel?"

"I am now. I'm doing what you sug-gested, reading the Journals first."

"I'm as new here as you are, you know. I mean in the graduate school."

A young man who was obviously waiting for Katherine came forward. Although the young man looked familiar, Roger did not recognize the name from his class list.

"I just sat in."

"You're going to audit?"

The man frowned. "I'm on the faculty."

His name was Henry Hadley, and he

taught English. Roger apologized pro-
fusely. "You're so young. You must be very
precocious."

Hadley's youth made his interest in Katherine understandable despite his faculty
status. But wasn't there a rule about frat-
ernization with students?

"Katherine isn't interested in my graduate
course."

"What are you teaching?"

"Comic heros of the fifties."

"Ah. Lucky Jim?"

"No, no. Comic book heroes."

"Haven't I seen you in the university archives?"

Hadley seemed reluctant to admit that he
sometimes worked there. It was Roger's favorite place. His first visit to the university
archives had been an event that would live
in the lore of that institution. He actually got
stuck in the door trying to get in and a monitor had to be called from the first floor of
the library to ease him the rest of the way
through. While this was going on, Roger
cheerfully told an anecdote about Chesterton, another man of size, an event that had
taken place during World War I. Chesterton
had been accosted by a patriotic matron on

the streets of London who demanded to know why he was not out at the front. "If you will go around to the side, madame," the writer replied, "you will see that I am."

Roger had roared at his own story and this, combined with a shove from the monitor, had effected his entrance into the archives. The allusion to Chesterton had provided the basis of friendship with an assistant archivist, Greg Whelan, who remarked that Chesterton had been a visitor to Notre Dame in the early thirties and that there were mementoes of that event in the archives. The head archivist seemed quite content to relinquish the massive visitor to Whelan and he led Professor Knight into his domain. For three hours, he had shown the new arrival some of the more precious items in the archives. On that occasion, Roger was particularly interested in anything that might shed light on Professor Frank O'Malley. Only after hours of easy repartee did it dawn on Greg that he was talking normally, nay, better than normally, speaking with the fluency and wit of his imagined conversations and all because he had in Professor Knight an appreciative listener.

In subsequent visits, Knight worked out what he called the "Heimlith maneuver," which enabled him to squeeze through the door on tiptoe, sideways, while holding his breath.

"It helps if I have only a light breakfast."

It was not an exaggeration to say that a day when Roger Knight came to the archives was for Greg Whelan a joyous one compared with which all other days were Lenten. And it was only with Roger Knight that the assistant archivist was able to converse as men are meant to converse. The rest of the time he was as mute as always, storing everything up so that he could tell it to himself aloud in the privacy of his own apartment.

Whelan had worked in the university archives on the sixth floor of the Hesburgh Library for some years now. He might have been said to be third in command if there had been any such thing as a chain of command. As a matter of fact, there was but one voice of authority, that of the head archivist herself, and Greg had made his peace with the notion that he was second, or perhaps third, violinist in a lesser orchestra. Lenore O'Day the head archivist was fair as well as imperious, highly skilled as well as peremptory, so it was largely a matter of noticing the good and ignoring the bad in her character. Of course everyone is a mélange of qualities taken from the two Pythagorean tables. Greg himself was no exception.

Far more difficult to cope with than the implication that he was a mere extension of his boss's arm and will was the condescension of most scholars who came to pursue their research in the archives. Still there was a small and secret satisfaction to be derived from their ignorance that he was every bit as educated as they. Indeed more so. His degrees told the story of his prolonged quest for a life's work. His doctorate was in history, from Columbia, but he had emerged into a job market that looked like a moonscape. For a year or two he was kept on as a course assistant and adjunct assistant professor, non-tenure-track appointments, but eventually this benefit to him was judged to be exploitation and his pittance had been taken away, leaving him to starve.

Like so many lost souls before him, he entered law school. His LSAT scores had

been maximum. He accepted the offer from
Virginia and was happy to get out of the
harsh north into the genteel south. The
placement director had gone over the job
situation with him and he had been assured
that he was not repeating his mistake in
history. Graduates were moving into lucra-
tive jobs in major firms with the most promising of futures opening before them.

Within three years all this had changed.
Firms were letting younger lawyers go, the
legal departments of corporations were cut-
ting back, seminars were being offered on
how to set up a law office. The one nega-
tive in Greg's choice of law had been his
almost pathological inability to communicate orally. He wrote with precision and
clarity and with great facility. After an encounter he could play out in his head elaborate scenarios in which he carried the
conversation with wit and insight, pith and
point, with what his enemies would call glib-
ness. But that was only in imagination. In
the real world, he was all but mute. He
could happily go through a day, two days,
an indefinite period, without speaking a
word to another person. Of course he
spoke to himself, eloquently, when alone,

telling himself such practice would break
the barrier and that soon he would be enun-
ciating like this in the real world.

With this handicap, it would have been
pointless to set up his own law office. He
went home to his parents and registered for
library science. It was this degree, as well
as his unusually impressive credentials,
that had won him the job in the Notre Dame
archives. Of course his background was
also resented, however unconsciously. But
if the archivist knew his accomplishments,
scholars did not. They treated him like a
librarian.

The appointment of Roger Knight as
Huneker Professor of Catholic Studies
came as an unexpected ray of light into the
cavelike existence of Gregory Whelan.

A cave six floors from ground level will
seem fanciful but the only windows in the
archives were in the archivist's office and
one workroom. By and large it was a place
of shelves, walls, artificial light. It could be
morning or night, summer or winter, stormy
or sunny, it was all one in the archives. In
winter, Greg arrived in the gloom and
stepped into the gloom again at night when
he came out of the library and crossed the

street to the lot where his economy stick-shifted car was parked. In winter, it would be encrusted with snow and it was an open question whether it would start; in summer, of course, it was not yet twilight when his work was done and his car was an oven that seemed to have stored up all the heat of the day, but this was almost welcome after the Arctic chill of the library. Summer and winter, Greg wore a thick sweater at work.

On Monday before the first home game, Greg was at work in the back of the archives when he heard the unmistakable sounds of Roger Knight's arrival. He hurried to the front to greet the professor. Knight took his arm as if for support but equally to lead him out of the earshot of others.

"Rockne," he whispered. "What do you have on Rockne?"

"Quite a lot," Greg said and seated himself at a computer. A few keys were depressed and on the screen a mass of information began to appear.

"What are you looking for, Professor?"

"Everything, Doctor." He had told Knight

something of his own educational background. "As long as you call me professor
I shall call you doctor."

He almost thought he should dissuade
Knight from this, lest colleagues find reason
for resentment in it.

"Everything?"

A confirming nod. Greg printed it out,
seven and a half pages of entries, and they
began systematically to go through the
Rockne holdings.

In imaginary conversation, Greg had
mocked the athletic reputation of the university. Mordant quips had drawn delighted
laughter from his fancied audience. It was
of course *de rigueur* for a certain kind of
professor to express disdain for varsity
sports, the attitude suggesting that once
the university had been a place where
everyone relentlessly pursued the truth and
nothing but the truth. However historically
unfounded, there was comfort in this for ef-
fete scholars who had never played games
and did not understand the games played
by those who could. Working with Roger
Knight, Greg found himself developing a
surprising passion for sports. The legendary Rockne, the butt of many condescend-

ing remarks, began to assume heroic proportions.

Their progress through the Rockne holdings seemed to move forward as toward a goal, but Knight would only say he was interested in everything. Then one day, when the head archivist had taken the afternoon off, they were having tea in her office and Knight mentioned what seemed to be the object of his interest.

"Rockne wrote a novel."

"The Four Winners."

"Of course you would know."

"It was reprinted recently."

"It was?"

"A local publisher, Icarus Press. Bruce Fingerhut. He learned his trade working with the university press and went on to form his own company."

"Was the reprint a success?"

"It was a well-kept secret."

"Where is Icarus Press?"

"Wherever companies go when they die."

"Bankrupt?"

"The victim of exorbitant interest rates during the Carter years."

"My interest is in the first edition. And its genesis."

"Then there are collateral holdings you will want to see."

"I should have confided in you sooner. What collateral holdings."

There were, Whelan said, the papers of F. X. Bourke, the legendary sportswriter whose career had paralleled the rise to prominence of Notre Dame athletics. He had been very close to Rockne.

"They played football together as students. With their inseparable friend, Arnold J. McInerny."

"The man to whom *The Four Winners* is dedicated?"

"He was killed in World War I. The Bourke papers have been bequeathed to the university, but the family has yet to release them. His study has been kept just as it was in his lifetime, almost a shrine."

"You have seen it?"

"Yes. In a fruitless attempt to find out when we could expect to receive the papers. The family house is almost a museum, with Bourke's study and library and papers as the centerpiece."

"Do you think they will renege on the old man's will?"

"Mr. Miranda, the university counsel, indicates that the university would be very reluctant to make a crusade to get those papers, not at the present time."

Pressed, Whelan told Roger of the theory of some that there was a kind of shame felt at the upper levels of the administration about the university's athletic reputation.

"But it is an excellent reputation."

"Too excellent. That is why they have stopped interfering with those who want to find faults with the program or demythologize its past. What do you know of Henry Hadley?"

Roger settled more comfortably on the sofa, three cushions of which were accommodating him.

"I have met him."

"Here?"

"He sat in on one of my classes."

"He is often here. He is a plague."

Hadley, Whelan explained, had conceived the idea of writing a novel about Knute Rockne.

"About Rockne?"

"He called it 'fictionalizing.' " The archivist could not prevent an expression of pain from moving across his face as clouds move across the sun. "His aim was to debunk Rockne, to expose him, to present him warts and all."

"To what purpose?"

Whelan shrugged and his shoulders seemed to lift the full burden of the world. At this point a thin figure in jeans, tennis shoes, and a faded sweatshirt with a hood which he had pulled over his head like a monk's cowl sidled into the archives. Roger did not at first recognize the man who had sat in on his seminar and gone off with Katherine George. He might otherwise have assumed that Hadley was with library maintenance.

"Ho," Hadley called.

Whelan made a jackknife bow, perhaps a gesture of contempt, and hurried away. The new arrival thrust his hand at Roger.

"How is your course on comic heroes going?"

A lopsided grin revealed uneven teeth. "You remember."

The hand that gripped Roger's was moist. "Now I am told that you are writing a novel."

Hadley withdrew his hand quickly, as if he thought it unsafe in Roger's. "Who told you that?" But his eyes went to the disappearing Whelan. "It's no secret."

"I should think not."

"George Gipp was a drunk. A delinquent. He was no Ronald Reagan." Hadley paused, looking as if he wanted to take back the last remark. "Rockne covered for him."

"I think all that is known."

"Yeah. Then why do they show incoming freshmen *The Knute Rockne Story*? Why do they promote the myth of the great coach and the fallen hero?"

"Your novel will challenge all that?"

"I'll give it a try."

"What do your colleagues think of your project?"

A sly look appeared in Hadley's eyes. "The book will be insurance. That's a bonus."

His reasoning was convoluted but in its way persuasive. By trashing the great legend of the university, Hadley hoped to disarm those who would deny him tenure. "Just let them try!" He would argue that any such decision was vengeful, a payback for his novel which by that time should be available in better bookstores everywhere.

"Except on campus. They won't let it be sold here."

He took pleasure from this anticipated boycott. Roger was beginning to understand Greg Whelan's attitude toward this young man and to be puzzled by Katherine George's apparent susceptibility to him. Hadley looked unshaven, but he might be growing a beard. There were rusty streaks on the front of his sweatshirt. He threw back the hood as if to expose his near baldness.

Behind Hadley the door opened again and Lenore came out. "I suppose you're talking about that crazy donor."

"Would you like to?" Roger asked.

"I'd like to get hold of his money so we could put up a decent building to house the archives. We're bursting at the seams."

"I know the feeling," Roger said, and everyone laughed as he knew they would. Being fat has its compensations. Eliciting laughter is addictive and Roger went on. "Perhaps Rockne could be buried in your building. That would be killing two birds with one Rock."

Only a punster loves his puns. The others groaned and the meeting dissolved. Roger went back to poring over the materials Greg had brought him.

5

Phil Knight's enthusiasm mounted as the season's first home game grew near. Considered in abstraction, it would perhaps be difficult to say what the attraction of football is to the adult mind. The sight of oversized bodies wearing bizarre protective gear, bubble helmets, and protruding face guards, crashing into one another on signal, knocking one another to the ground, might be said to lack even the finesse of wrestling. Of course such condescension is possible only to one who does not understand the game. Think of the players as chessmen, think of the plays as choreographed efforts to make grace and agility triumph over brawn and bulk, and the eye of the mind began to open to the beauty and intricacy of the contest. Easily the most aesthetically pleasing element of the game was the forward pass, the trademark of the redoubtable Rockne. Rockne himself had likened the game to war, with the opposing teams as armies, one attacking, the other defending. But he had stressed the major difference too. "Football is only a game."

The opportunity to watch Notre Dame play in its own stadium was a privilege indeed. And so when the day of the first home game dawned, both Phil and Roger awoke with the anticipation of excitement. For days, visitors had been descending on the campus, coming by private plane, by car, by chartered bus, by chauffeured limousine. The rooms in the Morris Inn had been reserved for years prior to the day, all the motels in the area were full of the seasonal clients for which they had principally been built. Restaurants, bars, fast-food places, did a land office business, and across the campus were scattered grills on which a variety of sausages and meats were cooked, sending up spires of sweet-smelling smoke. The paths around the lakes were crowded with visitors with an eye to exercise or simply for the lovely vista. At the grotto, people knelt to pray, perhaps asking for the favor of a victory that afternoon. Alumni clubs met, the years melted away as men and women visited the residence halls in which they had spent what they were all now certain had been the best years of their youth. And everywhere, surreptitiously, tickets for the game were being scalped. The bookstore emptied its racks and shelves of anything and everything bearing the monogram of the university. Some customers even found their way to the second floor, where books could be purchased.

In Roger's golf cart, the Knight brothers moved about the campus, enjoying the pageantry and panorama. The marching band formed in front of the main building to serenade the visitors and then the march to the stadium began. Pulses quickened as the clock ticked down to the initial kickoff. Roger, with the enthusiastic Philip and Father Carmody, went on foot the several hundred yards from the apartment, as eager as anyone for the game to begin. And so, eventually, it did. The first half was exciting but scoreless, except for two field goals, one by each side. There was tension in the stadium when the clock ran out, but with half the game left to play, no real anxiety.

It was during halftime that Father Carmody was called to the president's box and introduced to Marcus Bramble. Upon hearing that the new occupant of the Huneker Chair was at the game, the president invited the Knight brothers to a postgame reception at the Morris Inn. Perhaps he thought that proximity to the occupant of the Huneker benefaction would turn Bramble's mind to more academic uses of his money.

"How far is it?" Roger asked. He had been advised against driving his golf cart to the stadium and did not relish the walk back to the apartment.

"Oh, we'll be driven over."

"And back?"

"I'll arrange it. The benefactor who wishes to honor Knute Rockne will be there."

"Bramble," Roger said. "Marcus Bramble."

"Do you know him?"

"No, but I should like to. What precisely is it that he wants to give?"

"Ten million dollars."

"But for what purpose?"

"To honor Knute Rockne."

"But how?"

"That, Roger, you will have to ask our benefactor."

"I wonder if he knows of Rockne's novel."

"Novel!"

"Surely you know it, Father Carmody. *The Four Winners*. A prep school story set at Dulac Academy."

"I never heard of it."

Roger had learned that Father Carmody's memory was desultory. Roger had mentioned the novel to him several times.

The third quarter was an intense struggle between two teams of equal strength and determination, both relying chiefly on the ground game because of their untested quarterbacks. But in the fourth quarter, Notre Dame turned to a passing game. The first possession, the first play, Riggles the quarterback threw a forty-yard bomb that was carried into the end zone for a touch-

down. Riggles passed for a two-point conversion, and the score was 11-3. On the
kickoff, the return man bobbled the ball and
a Notre Dame man recovered. With the ball
on the seventeen-yard line, Riggles threw
a touchdown pass, again went for two
points, this time dropping back for a pass
and then carrying the ball into the end zone
himself when the defense fell back and left
the way clear for him. The score, 19-3. The
Notre Dame fans were ecstatic but the tri-
umphant rumble died away when the kickoff was returned to midfield and Stanford
reeled off three first downs and were at the
Notre Dame five-yard line. From there, a
quarterback draw carried them into the end
zone. They settled for a one-point conversion. 20-10.

There were eleven minutes to play when
Stanford made an onside kick and recovered it when a Notre Dame lineman decided to prove he had hands of lead.
Stanford unleashed an aerial attack and
within four minutes had scored another
touchdown. They went for two. 20-18. Notre Dame returned the kickoff and began
on their own twenty-five-yard line. The
passing game was forgotten and the time-

consuming ground game relied upon, slowly but relentlessly, to move Notre Dame down the field. On Stanford's twenty, the drive was stalled. It was fourth down and a yard to go. The quarterback called time-out and went to the sidelines to discuss it. When he came back in again, a signal that Notre Dame intended to go for a first down, the stands went crazy with excited approval. The teams lined up, the ball was snapped, but badly. The quarterback began to move forward, but without full control of the ball. A charging defenseman got through to him and the ball popped free. It rolled across the line of scrimmage and soon it seemed that every player on the field was part of the pile over the free ball. A Notre Dame player excitedly signaled that Notre Dame had recovered the ball but the officials were still busy trying to burrow to the bottom of the pile to see which team had controlled the ball. Finally the call was made. Stanford's ball.

A groan rose from the stands. Stanford had possession on its own eighteen with just over five minutes to play. Would they risk everything now? They stayed on the ground and once more began a slow, re-

lentless but time-consuming drive into Notre Dame territory. A penalty seemed
certain to alter the momentum, but once
more Stanford continued to burst through
the nearly exhausted Notre Dame defen-
sive line. With less than a minute left, the
ball was on the six-yard line and it was
fourth down with less than a yard to go. A
time-out was called. When it was over, Notre Dame called a time-out of its own. When
play resumed, Stanford had its kicker on
the field. They were going for a field goal,
which would give them three points, the
lead, and, barring a miracle, the game. But
first they had to make the field goal.

The stadium was all but silent as the two
teams lined up. The ball was snapped and
placed. The kicker came forward, he got his
foot into the ball, and it began the rising
trajectory that would take it over the goal-
post to victory. But suddenly the Notre
Dame center, extracting himself from the
grasp of an offensive tackle, leapt into the
air, arms extended. The ball hit his hand
and veered to the right but into the end
zone. Touchback. Notre Dame's ball on the
twenty. One series of downs took care of
the clock. The game was Notre Dame's.

There are many ways to win a football game, but this was one of the least satisfying. The crowd felt relief rather than triumph, and the cheering was perfunctory when the gun went off and the two teams milled around in midfield, scarcely believing the game was over. It was a game that neither team had lost and, despite the score, neither team had won.

The stands emptied and Roger was helped down the relatively steep stairway to the exit where the car that would take them to the Morris Inn was waiting.

Marcus Bramble, it turned out, was unaware of the Knute Rockne novel and was not particularly interested in it. He was a ruddy-faced man whose stadium coat had concealed his ample proportions. He tipped his head back and studied Roger after they had been introduced.

"Go ahead and say it," Roger suggested.

"Say what?"

"That I am not in fighting trim."

Bramble laughed, sloshing his drink. He took Roger's arm and pulled him toward a couch where they sat.

"I can't stand around like that anymore.

Not for any length of time. My legs won't take it."

"Did you play football here?"

Bramble tipped back his head again. "Not likely. I was a student assistant to the coach."

"Who was that?"

"Ara."

"And it is Rockne you want to honor?"

Bramble rolled within whispering range of Roger's ear. "My father was a student assistant under Leahy. He was an SOB to work for."

"Is that right?"

"He was a monk. He had a room in the firehouse, just a bed. That's where he stayed before big games. Football was his whole life."

"No time for fiction?"

Bramble waited. "You're asking me if he read?"

"I mentioned Knute Rockne's novel earlier."

"You were kidding, right?"

"Not at all. I discovered it in a second-hand bookstore a few years ago. Of course I bought it. I couldn't have been more surprised if I had learned that Rockne had authored a book on etiquette. I never thought of him as a novelist."

"He was a scientist," Bramble said insistently.

"The story is about college football."

"I don't believe it. Rockne, a novelist?" Bramble shook his head but took the precaution of holding his drink out in front of him so that it would not spill. Someone took it from him.

"Scotch?"

"Irish."

"Jameson?"

"Fine."

The president arrived before Bramble's drink.

"There are others I want you to meet." He looked at Roger reproachfully, as if he had been monopolizing the guest of honor.

"I want to hear more about that novel," Bramble said as he accepted the president's help in rising from the couch. "What's your name again, Professor?"

"Knight. With a silent *K*. As in Knute."

"Had enough?" Father Carmody asked, taking the place vacated by Bramble.

"Where's Phil?"

Phil was standing glass to glass with an

elegant woman with close-cropped hair and a nicely shaped head to go with it. The haircut gave her a fawnlike air as she looked fetchingly up at Phil over rimless glasses.

"With Madeline Rune. A trustee."

Philip brought Mrs. Rune with him, and Roger rose in an heroic effort to take her hand. Almost immediately Bramble was back. He scarcely acknowledged her when Phil introduced her.

"What is this silliness about Rockne?" she asked him.

"Nothing silly. I want to see him honored."

"Honored! Maybe they should rename the school."

"Something appropriate." The donor seemed intimidated by the mocking trustee.

"Knuter Dame, maybe."

"What have you got against Rockne?"

"Nothing. It's you who bothers me."

Roger separated the combatants and his gallantry was rewarded. Apparently Phil had told Mrs. Rune that they had miles to go before they slept. She offered to drive them back to their digs, but she wrinkled her nose as she said it. Or perhaps she was making a face at the departing Bramble.

"I hate that word. It sounds like a plot in Cedar Grove."

Cedar Grove was the cemetery just up Notre Dame Avenue, abutting what was left of the golf course. Father Carmody told Mrs. Rune that Roger was the Huneker Professor of Catholic Studies.

"That's a speciality now?"

"I am a law unto myself."

"How wonderful. Tell me about Catholic studies."

Father Carmody, keeping a step behind as they went out to Mrs. Rune's car, tried to tell her of Roger's book on Baron Corvo. But Roger suggested that he might offer a seminar on the writing of Knute Rockne.

Mrs. Rune's laughter lightly climbed the scale. "That ought to be soon done."

"I mean his literary work."

"Tell me you're not serious."

"You wouldn't believe how few people know of Knute Rockne's novel."

"Well, I am one of them. I never heard of it. And my family probably has the most extensive collection of Rockne memorabilia in existence."

"Marcus Bramble hadn't heard of it either."

Mrs. Rune made an impatient noise. "Why do people insist on telling the university how to use the money they give it?"

"You think a Rockne commemoration a mistake?"

She thought the whole thing was a publicity stunt, and she had told Marcus Bramble as much. He meant to draw attention to his professional teams. He was furious. So was the president. They were in the car now and she smiled up at the brothers, first at Phil, then at Roger. Father Carmody was on the facing seat. The driver, having been given instructions, closed the panel behind him.

"Now I want Professor Knight to tell me all these things I never knew before."

"Father Carmody is the man to ask. He has spent his life here at Notre Dame."

"For Rockne stories, you have to ask Quirk."

"Quirk?"

"Sebastian Quirk, CSC."

"Is he still alive?" Roger asked.

"You've heard of him?"

"Only what you told me, Father Carmody."

The old priest looked puzzled, as if he had forgotten telling Roger and Phil about the ancient terminally ill priest at Holy Cross House who was the last living link with prewar Notre Dame.

"Prewar?" Mrs. Rune asked, smiling prettily.

"Pre–World War II," Philip said. "Long before your time."

She squeezed his hand. "You must be a politician."

"Hardly that."

"What do you do?"

"I'm a private detective."

Her smile held as she waited to hear that Phil was telling a joke. "You're serious."

"Yes."

"I have had some terrible experiences with private detectives."

A silence in the car. It was not a remark easily followed up on. Philip got out a card and gave it to Mrs. Rune, offering to restore her faith in members of his profession. She tilted her head so as to find the appropriate region of her lenses through which to read it.

"There's no address."

"Roger and I live on campus temporarily."

She tapped her chin with the card, studying Phil, then gave it back to him. They had arrived at Holy Cross House.

"You're welcome to come in," Father Carmody said, as he backed out the door of the car.

"But I am taking them to dinner," Mrs. Rune cried. "I have reservations at the Carriage House."

"I will go with Father Carmody and Phil will go with you," Roger proposed.

"But you're so much more interesting than your brother." She smiled sweetly at Phil as she said this, gripping his arm. Roger hoped Phil would be safe with this predatory trustee.

"Can we pay a visit to Father Quirk?" Roger asked as the long car rolled away.

"That's why I asked you. No telling how long he'll last."

6

Holy cross house, a low one-storied building of buff brick and blue decoration, was located on the north side of St. Joseph Lake but was not accessible from the campus. One had to drive along the northern boundary of the campus, on Douglas Road, in order to gain access to it. To call the place an infirmary would be misleading, to call it a retirement home was closer to the mark. What everyone understood was that this was the last stop in this Vale of Tears for members of the congregation. There were one or two younger men in their sixties in residence, recovering from one operation or another, but by and large the rooms in the corridors that rayed out from the nurses' station were filled with terminal cases.

A bulletin board across from the counter of the nurses' station was covered with cards bearing the photographs of priests and brothers. Closer inspection revealed that these were cards commemorating the death and burial of the man in question.

Father Carmody paused and let his eye roam over the display, shaking his head.

"I can't believe some of these men are dead."

" 'I had not thought death had undone so many.' "

Father Carmody turned and waited.

"Dante."

"Of course."

"Or T. S. Eliot."

"Aren't you sure?"

But Carmody's eye was drawn back to the board and he began to point out some of his old friends, saying how much he wished Roger had known them.

"Sheedy there. In many ways an odd man but he was an omnivorous reader. He was always recommending books he had just finished." Carmody closed his eyes and smiled. "*The Tichbourne Claimant* was one. And *Catch 22*. He put me on to those. He was dean for years."

"Dean of what?"

"Arts and Letters. I don't think we've had one since who read."

"Ah well, deans."

Carmody called out to the nurse that they were going to visit Quirk.

"He's sleeping, Father."

"We'll wake him up."

"You'll wake everyone in the house talking so loud. I gave him a pill."

Carmody ignored this. He had the aged celibate's slightly condescending attitude toward females. That one should actually have authority over him or any other male was unthinkable to him. It was not that he had formed the thought and rejected it. His mind was unable to accommodate it.

They shuffled off down a corridor lined with rooms, most with their doors open. The beds were for the most part hospital beds and on them lay cadaverous occupants, pale of skin, sharp of features, eyes closed. From time to time, a more lively resident came into view, looking sharply out at them. It occurred to Roger that he and Father Carmody represented the pageant of the outside world to those curious eyes.

Father Sebastian Quirk was at the end of the corridor in a room that had two windows, one of which looked out at the lake and at the university buildings rising above the trees on the opposite shore. He sat in a chair with his hands laid lightly on its arms, his body wrapped in an oversized blue and gold robe. Thin white hair rose from his skull like an angel's aureole in a Renaissance painting. His smile as he looked up at them was genuine, however artificial the dentures.

"Father Quirk . . . ," Carmody began, but an ancient hand rose to stay him.

Roger concluded that the large plug in the priest's ear was not a hearing aid in the usual sense. He was listening to the radio.

"They are replaying the game."

"We'll come back another time," Father Carmody said petulantly.

"Oh no no no." The thought of losing visitors seemed to be more painful than not hearing a replay of the game so recently ended in victory. Quirk removed the ear plug in a dramatic gesture of self-denial.

"There is a televised replay tomorrow morning," he explained to Roger.

Carmody drew up some straight-back chairs and put Roger knee to knee with the ancient Father Quirk.

"This is Roger Knight, Sebastian. He is the Huneker Professor of Catholic Studies. This is his first year. . . ."

"I can hear, I can hear," Quirk said impatiently. Carmody was speaking in a very loud voice and forming each word with a precision that would have delighted a teacher of elocution. "Did you go to Notre Dame?"

"Princeton."

"Presbyterian?"

"I converted to Catholicism there."

"Good man. Fitzgerald lost his faith there."

"Have you heard about Marcus Bramble's ten-million-dollar gift, Father? To honor Rockne."

"What's he want to do?"

"That's unclear. Where is Rockne buried, Father?"

"Highland Cemetery. Over on Portage Avenue. Highland is on one side, Riverview on the other."

"Why is he buried way over there?"

"It's not a mile away."

"As the crow flies. Or airplanes landing at the Michiana Airport."

"I hate that word."

"Illiana," Carmody said, as one might scape his nails on a blackboard.

"Worse, worse."

"Tex Mex," Roger offered. He realized he was hungry. The hors d'oeuvres at the reception were all that stood between him and the hot dogs and popcorn he had consumed during the game. Thoughts of Phil settling down to a grand dinner with Mrs. Rune came and went.

"Lots of lay faculty are buried over there." He looked wickedly up at Roger. "Dead ones, of course."

"Bramble sounds as if he wants Rockne's grave relocated."

Father Quirk thought of that. "Not a bad idea. It's hard to find the place in Highland."

"More are buried in Cedar Grove," Carmody mused.

"All in Cedar Grove are buried."

"Father Quirk taught logic."

"Not if no one learned it."

"Largely to athletes," Father Carmody added.

Roger was given the story later. Sebastian Quirk had been an undergraduate during the golden Rockne years. He entered the novitiate, studied theology in Washington, and earned a master's in philosophy before returning to Notre Dame. It was during his early years on the faculty that Knute Rockne had died in a Kansas plane crash. The two beacons of Sebastian Quirk's life had been Father Edward Sorin, the founder of Notre Dame, and Knute Rockne. He assigned himself the special mission of assuring that athletes did not fall behind in their studies because of the time devoted to sports. His courses became favorites of athletes, particularly of football players. From Father Quirk students learned the tradition and lore of Notre Dame and he did not hesitate to give pride of place to athletics.

"A sound mind in a sound body," the old priest cried, as if he had just thought it up. *"Mens sana in corpore sano."*

"There was a cigarette named Sano," Carmody remarked.

"That is the sentiment expressed in *The Four Winners*."

"You've read it?" Father Quirk seemed delighted.

"Yes."

"What did you think?"

Roger gave it some more thought. "It is good of its kind. Stover at Yale."

"The model was Father Francis Finn."

"Father Finn. *Tom Playfair. Percy Wynn*. Wonderful books."

"I don't know them," Carmody said.

Quirk ignored him. "Finn was a Jesuit, but even so."

"Father, you are the first one I've mentioned it to who knew of Rockne's novel."

Quirk lifted his eyes as if in comment on these dark times. "During orientation freshmen are shown the movie. They should be given the book as well."

If the Notre Dame of *The Knute Rockne Story*, starring Pat O'Brien as the coach and Ronald Reagan as the Gipper, was different from the contemporary university, the world of *The Four Winners* was more distant still.

"Bramble should finance a new edition."

"I never heard of it, Sebastian."

"More shame you. There's a copy on the shelf."

Father Carmody picked up a slim blue volume and read its spine. "Devin Adair."

"Good publisher," Quirk said emphatically. "And they were delighted to get the book."

"Did it sell well?"

"You'd have to check with accounting." Father Quirk leaned forward and whispered to his guests. "Bourke helped him write it."

"Which Bourke?"

"We did have lots of them. Bourkes." The ancient priest's smile reappeared. "Who was it that said we were too-Bourkelar?" He cackled at the remembered joke.

"Is he dead?"

Sebastian Quirk seemed suddenly to be seeing them from the other side of a veil.

"They're all dead."

7

The carriage house restaurant was located in a restored building that had indeed once been a carriage house. It was a delightful surprise to Philip, who wondered how anyone would know that such a place was located so far out in the country like this. For answer, Mrs. Rune looked around. There was not an empty table.

"It is a favorite place to come after a game."

"You had a reservation?"

"Of course."

Roger did not drink, so it was a rare pleasure for Phil to order the wine. The drinks they had at the reception were sufficient preprandial refreshment.

"Preprandial?"

"Roger talks like that. My vocabulary expands by osmosis."

"I'll have to remember that."

"What did you mean about private detectives?"

She looked at him in silence for a long minute. "There is a Mr. Rune."

"Ah."

"We are separated. Informally. I became a practicing Catholic again to marry him and now he wants a divorce. Maybe even an annulment."

"There's someone else?"

Her laughter was not happy. "That sounds singular. Some ones is more like it."

Philip was beginning to regret having accepted her invitation. But then it was Roger who had accepted for him, as if wanting to be free of him for a time. The prospect of an evening with an attractive woman had not been repellant, but Mrs. Rune now sounded like a client he would not accept. A private detective has forced upon him the realization that most people are governed by their loins—another Rogeresque expression. The alternating attraction and repulsion of the opposite sex, the childish changing of partners for the most trivial reasons, lay at the basis of most of the trouble in the world. It certainly generated the bulk of a private investigator's business. Among the clichés and truisms that increasingly clicked with truth was the oldest of them all: *Cherchez la femme*. Or *l'homme*, in the case of the *femme*. Mrs. Rune had succeeded, with a few offhand remarks, in making herself ordinary.

"Actually, he would prefer me dead. That would fulfill the bargain."

Philip looked receptive.

" 'As long as you both shall live.' It was a solemn thing, marrying Stanley in the church as a returned Catholic. This was to be for keeps and we both knew it. Then."

"Marriage should be for keeps."

"Of course it should. But half the time I wish he was dead."

It would have been cynical to tell her that this was the sentiment of many married people, at least some of the time. He was never sure whether the spouses he met in the line of duty were a fair sample of all the others. What he remembered of the parents he and Roger had lost in childhood suggested otherwise. He found himself telling Madeline Rune about himself and Roger, if only to get off the topic of her marital troubles.

Ten years older than Roger, Phil had willingly taken on the role of foster parent as well as older brother. But it was only in practical matters that any sense of superiority to Roger persisted. Very early on it had become clear that Roger had a phenomenal mental capacity. It took some time before Roger himself learned that others his age were not pretending ignorance in school in order to tease the teacher. He stopped seeing how low he could score on tests and soon the truth was known.

It was a frightening thought that a boy of ten was ready for college. Had Phil been able to afford it, he would have hired tutors, to spare Roger the socially demanding experience of being a child among adults on campus, adults with mental capacities far less than his own. Roger grazed over the offerings, effortlessly following courses in science and engineering, architecture and business, these interests radiating out from his permanent love for the liberal arts. After four years he had fulfilled requirements for a dozen majors and the question became what was his central interest. In graduate school he would have to choose. History beckoned and so did literature, but a reading of the *Tractatus* determined Roger to go into philosophy.

"You are impressed by Wittgenstein?"

"Fascinated. Of course the *Tractatus* is nonsense."

"Nonsense?"

"It is all grounded on a *petitio principii.*"

The board named to interview this unusual candidate was fascinated by such heresy. It was a time when it was unheard of to dismiss Wittgenstein in this way. Roger likened the Austrian's work to Russell's philosophy of logical atomism.

"Do you think they are the same?"

"Russell is far less persuasive, but then he lacks the note of Teutonic mystery. Of course he is logically more interesting."

Roger was admitted. He did well, however against the grain his thinking went. The mandatory scoffing at things medieval turned him to Ockham and Scotus. Fortunately his curiosity survived these two and he went on to Thomas Aquinas. He came to think that western civilization had been on a downhill slide since the thirteenth century, philosophically speaking. His dissertation was a 125-page demolition of the *Critique of Pure Reason*. He became a Catholic at the age of eighteen, an autodidact here as in much else. He had pored over the catechism with a docility that shamed the priest who gave him instructions. The priest seemed to think Roger had come to hear of his disagreements with the Pope. By the time Roger was baptized, the priest had become an ultramontane, more papal than the pope.

"Moderation is foreign to him," Roger observed to Phil. "I fear for him. We must remember him in our prayers."

Roger made no effort to proselytize his brother, which sometimes irked Phil, as if he were considered beyond the pale. People assumed he was a Catholic too and he had stopped correcting the impression. But at table with Madeline Rune he made his status clear.

"So what are you?"

He shrugged. "I take Roger to Mass. He can't drive himself."

"You're more Catholic than Stanley."

"That may be more of a comment on Stanley than on me."

"You're right about that. You're making me sorry we didn't insist that Roger come along."

"Oh, he will be much happier with Father Quirk."

"That's not very flattering."

"Roger is not always discerning."

She smiled as if he had caressed her. "Are you married?"

"No."

"Never?"

"Not yet."

"I advise against it. People get married because they think they are expected to. After a certain age, it is more trouble for a woman to be single than married. Perhaps things are changing in that respect, but I don't really think so."

"I can't believe that you just wandered into marriage."

"You're right. I didn't. I was swept off my feet. Stanley played football and my family's connection with Notre Dame athletics goes back to the Ice Age. He could have played professionally, but he was eager to begin his legal career."

"In South Bend?"

"Good heavens no. Chicago."

"You seem to know the locale."

"I grew up here. And we lived here while he went through law school. I kept the family house."

"Where do you live in Chicago?"

She smiled. "I am telling you all my secrets."

"Is where you live a secret?"

"I have moved back to South Bend." She waited for his reaction and when he said nothing grew serious. "That was a mistake. What do I expect, for time to go backward so I can be a girl again and start over? It doesn't work like that, does it?"

"How is your family connected with Notre Dame athletics?"

"My mother was a Bourke."

She seemed to think that was explanation enough, but when Philip did not react she told him about her maternal grandfather, Francis Xavier Bourke. "He went back to Rockne, to before; they played football together as undergraduates. F. X. became a sportswriter, right here in South Bend. He turned down offers from Chicago and New York to stay here. Notre Dame football was his beat and he knew it. My uncle also played." She fell silent. "He played football and graduated and went to Korea and died. My grandfather never quite recovered from that. Uncle Len was going to do all the things my grandfather only wrote about. My grandfather retired and lost himself in the past."

"How so?"

"His workroom at home was a private museum. He never threw anything away. He relived every Notre Dame game he had ever seen. He knew every play, the scores at halftime, the players. But he wouldn't go to another game. I guess I'm taking after him, moving back here, hanging around the university. My cousins hate me for it."

"Why?"

"They want to turn the house into a museum, a private museum. They think it would pay. It wouldn't. The whole lot is to go to Notre Dame."

"You said 'hanging around the university.' Aren't you a trustee?"

"How often do you think trustees come to campus?"

"What will happen to your grandfather's stuff?"

"It will go to the Notre Dame archives. Some is already there."

"Does Marcus Bramble know of it?"

"Bramble! Why don't we all grow up and stop idolizing coaches and athletes?"

"I wouldn't have missed today's game for anything."

She smiled. "Neither would I." She grew serious. "I think I want to hire you."

"No you don't."

"I don't think so or I don't want to?"

"Both."

"I think Stanley intends to kill me."

Everything she had said to this point led Philip to think this was the remark of a scorned woman whose sophistication muted her reaction in one sense and exaggerated it in another. No woman takes easily the realization that she is being set aside for another. And it had become clear that Madeline did not believe Stanley simply wanted to play the field. Her rival was a young woman in her twenties, golden-haired, athletic, daughter of a Notre Dame professor.

"Does she live in South Bend?"

"With Dad," Madeline said with irony.

"She sounds safe."

"It's me I'm worried about."

"Has he threatened you?"

"Of course he has. And I've threatened him. Oh, we are a pair, Stanley and I. God have mercy on us."

"Amen."

"You sound as if you mean that."

"I do."

"Thank you."

On that odd note their dinner ended. Her driver had eaten and stood outside smoking a cigarette and contemplating the starry sky above. They rode back to campus in pensive silence.

"I *am* worried," she said.

"Most such threats are idle."

"That's reassuring."

"Is your husband in danger from you?"

She laughed a joyless laugh. "I see what you mean."

She kissed him impulsively on the cheek before he got out of the car at the apartment.

"You are a very sympathetic man. You really listen. I wish I had kept your card."

Reluctantly he gave her another. He felt like a hypocrite when he pressed it into her hand, got out of the car, and closed the door.

The car drove off into the night, heading toward campus.

8

When Norm Sheuer came up the drive of the Bourke house at five-thirty Sunday morning he was about as awake as he ever was when delivering the Chicago papers to South Bend subscribers. Beside him, Rose checked off each delivery. She looked as sleepy as he felt. The trick on Sundays was to deliver the papers without coming fully awake and then get back home and pile into bed until the first NFL game came on.

"What's that?" Rose asked, looking toward the house. Norm had shoved the gear into park and was opening the driver's door. He always placed this paper carefully inside the front screen door, happy to have the address back on his route.

"What's what?"

"Lying on the porch."

There was a woman lying facedown on the porch floor, one foot preventing the screen door from closing, as if she hadn't quite made it outside. The back of her head was a mess. It was Madeline Rune. Norm's first impulse was to help her up, but Rose was beside him now.

"Don't touch her!"

"Mrs. Rune?" he called.

"Norm, she's dead."

This amateur opinion was confirmed by the paramedics who arrived ten minutes later with siren screaming, summoned by Rose on the cellular phone. Norm and Rose were soon pushed aside, and after fifteen minutes during which one patrol car after another roared up the driveway, they managed to free their van and continue delivering papers.

"Why did you leave the scene?" Officer Jensen demanded when he came pounding on their door during the first quarter of the first NFL game of the afternoon. Chicago fumbled the ball then and Norm glared at the cop as if his arrival had caused it. Jensen's eye went to the screen.

"What's the score?"

He watched for a while standing and then took a chair. Rose gave him a cup of coffee. At halftime he asked Norm about the scene he had come upon at the Bourke house. The place was still called that, after the sportswriter who had built it and raised his family in it.

"I took some pictures," Rose said.

"You did!"

Rose nodded. In high school she had won a prize for a photograph that had been printed in the *South Bend Tribune* and ever since she had considered herself a photographer in search of a subject. She always had a camera in purse or pocket.

"She's pretty good," Norm said.

"Do you want me to turn them in?"

Jensen thought about it, then shook his head. "We took lots of pictures after you left."

"What happened to her?"

Jensen looked wise. "We're still looking into that."

                    *   *   *

The on-site investigation was nearly done when it was discovered that there was someone in the house. Mrs. Taylor, teeth out, hearing aids on the table beside her, hair all done up in rollers, rose from her bed like a hypnotist's subject when the police pushed open the door of her third floor room and wakened her. With one hand she pulled the bedclothes well up under her seventy-eight-year-old chin, with the other she snatched her denture from the table and, ducking her head, got it in place. Then she screamed.

She was the housekeeper/cook and she had slept through whatever had happened the night before to the lady of the house. When she learned that Maddie, as she called her, was dead she swung her legs out of bed and seemed to be performing a little dance as her toes searched for her mules. She pointed to a robe thrown over a chair and this was handed to her. Risen and wrapped in her Indian blanket robe, she regained her dignity.

"Take me to her."

That meant going to the morgue when they decided that Mrs. Taylor could make the identification. There might just as well be some official point to acceding to her peremptory request that she be shown the body of her employer.

"God bless her soul," she said solemnly, looking at the lifeless body. "She might be sleeping. Except for the color." She reached out to touch the face of the deceased, but the coroner stopped her.

Whether Mrs. Taylor would have come along with them if they had told her they wanted to question her was a toss-up.

"Had she expressed any fear?" Detective Waring asked. Waring had shown up at the murder site at seven and, when the victim's purse was examined, took the private investigator's business card with the phone number penciled on the back. Spindler, Waring's assistant, asked Mrs. Taylor if she could tell them anything that would shed any light on what had happened to Madeline Rune.

"Have you talked to Mister?"

"You think he did this?"

"I think you should talk to him."

Madeline Rune's death was not of course reported in the Sunday morning paper. It had happened too late for that. The Knight brothers first heard of it in a call from Father Carmody. Minutes later another call came, from the South Bend police. Did Philip know Mrs. Madeline Rune?

"I met her yesterday."

"When did you last see her."

"We had dinner together."

"My name is Detective Waring. Something has happened to Mrs. Rune."

"I know. She's dead."

"How did you know that?"

"Father Carmody just called to tell me. How did she die?"

"I'd like to talk to you."

When Father Carmody's call came, Philip had been telling Roger about his dinner with Madeline Rune and of her interest in the fact that he was a private investigator.

"Had you taken her as a client?" Roger asked when Philip put down the receiver after Waring's call.

Philip made a face. "I thought she was exaggerating."

"What was she like?"

"Was. That's hard to believe."

"She was attractive."

"Yes. And full of secrets."

Much about the Runes that had been secret, or at least private, was to become
public knowledge during the following days.

When they separated, Madeline had
moved back into the family home overlooking the St. Joseph River north of South
Bend, a house she had never been able to
bring herself to sell. Like most other things,
it had been the occasion of misunderstand-
ing between her and Stanley. She had assumed that he liked having it waiting for
them on their frequent visits to South Bend.
He had always emitted a sigh when they
turned into the driveway and he would stop
the car as if to admire the majestic sweep
of lawn, with the house just visible through
the trees.

"I hate the goddamn place," he insisted
later. "It's haunted."

"You love it!"

"It's a white elephant. You couldn't give
it away."

She was speechless with surprise and
then with rage. Give away the house her
grandfather had built? She would never sell
it, not now. The spaciousness of the house
and all those rooms daunted her and she

filled the place with geegaws in a losing attempt to put her own stamp on the house. Stanley was right about one thing. The house *was* haunted. The ghost of her grandfather inhabited it. It was Stanley who called them geegaws. He had liked that word because it seemed to contain a built-in sneer. He told her that he hated the serpentine country road leading to the house and the long, icy driveway in winter, to say nothing of the leaves that fell for months each autumn, necessitating crew after crew of unemployables milling around the property. Stanley was always certain they were sizing the place up for a later clandestine visit. They had always had graduate students living in the apartment over the garage, rent-free but responsible for the house in the absence of the Runes. Madeline would never have admitted to Stanley that she too had hated the huge, drafty house and the rooms that never looked lived in, no matter how many geegaws she put in them. She had rejected the thought of a condo in South Bend, and would never have lived in one of the developments in the Granger sprawl to the northeast of town. It was the view of the river that drew her back to the ancestral house. The house was set high on an overlooking bank and there was the consoling ceaseless northward flow of the St. Joseph River to persuade her that nothing was so awful that it would not pass.

Her return to the house had been resented by her cousins, Jim and Carey Walker, though they had absolutely no claim on the property.

"The F. X. Bourke museum," Jim would say and Carey would nod agreement. "It would coin money. All that Rockne stuff, all the Notre Dame stuff. Think of the people who would want to stop by on weekends when Notre Dame plays at home."

"It's too out of the way. Besides, there would have to be a staff."

Jim let Carey say it. They were proposing themselves as caretakers/managers. They wouldn't ask for a salary, just a percentage of profits.

"It all belongs to Notre Dame."

"Then why is it still in the house?"

"I am going to turn it over to the archives. That's what F. X. wanted."

What would the house be like if it could be exorcised of the ghost of F. X. Bourke?

* * *

"What did she have on?" Phil asked Waring.

"Why do you ask?" Waring might have been a podiatrist or a lesser clerk in a bank. His white shirt was very clean and very starched and the knot of his tie small. He blinked, perhaps because of the discomfort of contacts.

"To get an answer."

The answer indicated that she was still dressed as she had been at the Carriage House.

"Did she give any indication that something like this might happen?" Waring asked.

"Something like what?"

"It is almost certain that she was killed."

"Almost?"

"To the naked eye. The coroner's report will decide that."

"Do you doubt it?"

"No."

"Have you talked to her husband?"

"Aren't they divorced?"

"Separated."

"How long have you known her?"

"Known her? I just met the lady yesterday, after the game."

"She tell you all about herself?"

"I am a private investigator, Waring."

Waring blinked and nodded. "She had your card in her purse. Was she your client?"

"She wanted to hire me."

"Why?"

"She feared that what has happened might happen."

"The husband?"

Phil nodded. Waring looked around the apartment.

"How come you live on campus?"

"My brother is on the faculty."

"I didn't know faculty lived on campus."

"It's a special arrangement," Roger said, pulling the footstool on which he sat closer to the detective. "Actually, I am just a visiting professor, technically. This is temporary housing."

"Are you retired?" Waring asked Phil.

"Oh no. I take a client now and then."

"Now and then?"

Phil explained about New York and moving to Rye and the 800 number. Waring lis-

tened carefully as if he were casting himself
for the role Phil described.

"Did Mrs. Rune call your number?"

"I met her at the president's party. She
was a university trustee."

Waring sat back in alarm. His expression
indicated that anything involving the university posed special problems of delicacy
for one in his position. This visit to the Hesburgh Center had not entailed going
through a campus entry.

"Can I use your phone?"

Roger eavesdropped shamelessly. His
hunch was right. Waring wanted the mayor
to be told they had a Notre Dame problem.

"The Rune woman? She was a trustee.
No, not at the jail, for God's sake. Like on
the board."

Waring hung up and had a thought. "Is
her husband a trustee too?"

"I don't know."

"Tell me what she said about her husband."

"Look, Waring, I had dinner with her, she
dropped me off here before eleven. That's
it. If I were you I would want to talk to the
husband."

"That's being done."

The phone rang while Waring was still there and the detective picked it up as if it were for him.

"Just a minute." He handed the phone to Roger.

"Was that your brother?" a voice roared in Roger's ear.

"Mr. Bramble?"

"Marcus. Marcus. Look, I should have asked you last night. Can you have breakfast with me?"

"We haven't been to Mass yet."

"When do you go?"

"There's a nine o'clock at Holy Cross House."

"Can I go?"

Roger hesitated only long enough to see the advantages of being picked up by Bramble and driven to the retirement home. He cupped the phone and was explaining the arrangements to Phil when Waring intervened.

"I'm going to the murder scene. Care to come along?" Waring asked. One detective to another. Phil agreed.

"It's a deal," Roger said into the phone.

"Perfect. We have things to talk about."

Apparently not Madeline Rune. But it was unlikely that Marcus Bramble would have heard of what had happened to her. Roger told Bramble how to get to where he was.

"Who was that?" Waring asked, then made a gesture with his hand. "Of course you don't have to answer that."

"A man who was here for the football game. He's a great football fan."

"Did you see the game?"

"Yes?"

Philip wondering how much of what Madeline Rune had told him was now known to the police, asked Waring if a motive had been discovered.

"Marriage."

Phil laughed. "Why would he kill her?"

"Spouses don't need any reason beyond the fact that they are sick to death of one another."

Roger thought about that. It wasn't that he doubted what Waring said, he had shared some of the incidents that might have brought Phil to the same apparently cynical conclusion. To wonder about something is not to doubt that it is true but why it is true. Everything he remembered and everything Phil had told him of their parents

suggested a far different sort of relationship, the kind one would like to think is the
normal marital situation. But many people
were obviously married to their worst enemy.

Roger said, "Did the Runes have children, Phil?"

"She didn't mention any."

"Then they must not have any."

Children seemed a buffer and bond that
carried two people beyond the intensity of
the one-on-one of husband and wife. Father and mother are more expansive roles
and leave less room for the annoyances
that can end with the man in one city and
the wife in another.

Waring's invitation to Phil to come along
with him to Niles was a blessing of sorts.
Phil could not be a mere observer of what
had happened to Madeline Rune. Perhaps
he was not the last one to see her, but it
looked as if he was the last one she had
been with. He had found the woman attractive, that seemed clear, but underlying
everything was the sense of having been
himself somehow attacked.

"I wonder if we were being followed."

"By the husband?" Visions of tabloid scenes danced before Roger's eyes. Estranged husband assaults wife's date.

"By whoever did it."

9

The Chapel at Holy Cross House was parallel to a corridor and had a narrow, scrunched look. A younger priest in his late sixties said the Mass, but the ancient priests all wore stoles and more or less concelebrated. Sebastian Quirk wheeled in, his chair powered by himself rather than electricity, smartly turned his chair 360 degrees, backed into a corner, and waited as if for applause. None of the other priests seemed to notice him. A very elaborate stole was draped over his hunched shoulders with what seemed to be shamrocks embroidered on it.

"Quirk," Roger said to Bramble and then, to avoid ambiguity, "Father Quirk."

Bramble nodded, but his expression was puzzled.

"He knew Rockne."

A look of reverence spread over Marcus Bramble's face at this reminder of his true religion. The dogmas and creed of his faith claimed his allegiance, but in his heart being a Catholic and being an alumnus of Notre Dame pretty much came to the same thing. Others might regard the athletic contests in which the university teams engaged as mere games. For Bramble they meant more, much more. They were theological tournaments. Victory was equivalent to a proof of the faith. A loss was like a plague laid upon Egypt. When they occurred, he then sought the source of the Lord's displeasure in the policies of the university administration. His determination to give ten million dollars for a fitting memorial to Knute Rockne was something of a propitiatory gift. It had been half a dozen years since Notre Dame had been acknowledged as the national champion in football. Bramble stressed "acknowledged," since all fairminded persons knew that at least twice

Notre Dame had been jobbed out of the title by the forces of bigotry. To be able to lay his eyes on a man who had laid his eyes on the venerated Rockne was a spiritual experience. Throughout the Mass he stretched and changed positions, never letting Father Quirk out of his sight.

"I want to talk to him," he whispered hoarsely.

"Father Carmody may ask us to breakfast here."

"With Father Quirk?"

"I'll ask."

Bramble's eyes rolled upward in a silent prayer of thanksgiving. At the moment, if asked, he would have doubled his proposed gift to the university.

During the canon, those mobile enough to do so went forward and ringed the celebrant, frowning over the cards that contained the latest variation on the Mass prayers they had said all their lives. Of course, these men would have said Mass in Latin until Vatican II had swept all that away in the interests of a constantly changing, progressively more banal Englishing of the sacred text. The one in use in the chapel of Holy Cross, although several versions prior to the latest, was bad enough.

Roger prayed for the repose of the soul of Madeline Rune, the attractive woman who had been so lively and humorous just the night before, only hours before she met her maker. His beliefs about the afterlife did not supply Roger with images and he did not try to picture the reality into which Madeline's soul had been so abruptly introduced. Her death seemed an interruption, a surprise, but all men are mortal and the essence of the Christian faith was that this life is but a preparation for an eternal duration of either blissful union with God or the eternal loss of Him. After receiving communion, he whispered a *De profundis* for Madeline.

"Why don't you say Mass in Latin?" Roger asked Father Carmody in the hallway afterward. Beside him, Bramble jittered nervously, one eye on the door through which Father Quirk would exit from the chapel, the other on Roger, willing him to put the crucial question.

"The house is crawling with liberals."

"That's hard to believe."

"It's harder to live with."

It was difficult to think of the dozen old priests who had been in chapel as holding strongly to any views about the shifting sands of the liturgy. Roger would have thought nostalgia alone might prompt the desire to say the Mass in old age as one had said it in youth.

"Not many of them were very good at Latin."

"We met yesterday," Bramble burst out, extending his hand to Carmody. "Marcus Bramble."

Carmody backed away as he recognized the benefactor. His expression suggested that he regarded Bramble as like the Pharisee in the Gospel, tinkling a bell to call attention to his almsgiving, ostentatious generosity. Roger wondered if the priest thought Bramble's vainglory vitiated the giving. Or did he resent this appropriation of the school's sacred lore by an outsider? Bramble might be an alumnus but he was still an outsider.

"I am going to breakfast with Mr. Bramble, Father Carmody."

"That's too bad. I was going to ask you to join me."

"We'd be glad to," Bramble cried, startling Father Carmody.

"Could Father Quirk join us?" Roger moved to the side, lest Bramble kiss him in gratitude.

As if on cue, Father Quirk wheeled out of the chapel. Like a teenager at the sight of a rock star, like steel filings in the presence of a magnet, Bramble moved toward the object of his devotion, his feet seeming to float above the surface of the floor. Father Quirk turned quickly, fearful of a collision. Bramble grabbed the handles at the back of the chair and swung Quirk around again. The old man rocked sideways and a spidery hand gripped the arm of the chair. A little bleat of fear escaped him and he looked back at Bramble, terrified.

"Oh my God, Father, I'm sorry. Are you all right? What a stupid thing to do. Here, let me get you settled better."

Quirk bleated again as Bramble made a move to square him in the chair. Carmody came forward and calmed his older colleague. Quirk settled down when Roger came into view and Carmody told him of the emerging plans for breakfast. With some reluctance, Quirk allowed himself to be rolled into the refectory. Bramble took up his post at the side of Quirk's chair and had to be persuaded to sit down. Phil moved so that the benefactor could sit close to Quirk. The old priest continued to eye Bramble with wariness.

"This is the man who has offered the university a large sum of money to put up a fitting memorial to Knute Rockne," Roger explained. For the first time, Quirk was at ease.

"I knew the Rock."

"You're the last man on earth who can say that," Carmody said, and there was no lugubrious note in his voice.

"Tell me about him," Bramble breathed.

The last hint of reluctance left the old priest. His status vis-à-vis Rockne was unquestioned, his fund of anecdotes unmatchable, and of course unverifiable, but the fact was that he was daily surrounded by men who were either beyond caring or who had heard his standard repertoire more often than they had wanted. He was in the position of a storyteller without an audience. Marcus Bramble was a godsend.

"How much do you know of the Rock?" Quirk asked.

"I want to hear everything."

The years seemed to fall from Father Quirk's shoulders and he sat more erectly in his chair. A dignity, even sacredness came over him, as he assumed the task of a bard passing on the oral traditions of the tribe to the young.

On more than one occasion, Roger was struck by the similarity of an anecdote with an episode in *The Four Winners*. When he mentioned this, Bramble looked at him impatiently.

Coffee was poured, poached eggs peppered and salted, then more coffee was poured and sweet rolls were eaten. There was an anticipatory air, as they all looked ahead to Father Quirk's account. The other tables had filled when the group sat down but were now emptying. The question of Marcus Bramble's gift came up.

"What are you proposing?" Quirk asked.

"Why is Rockne buried in Highland Cemetery?"

"That was the family's decision."

"But why not on campus?"

"How much do you know of Mrs. Rockne?"

Bramble's impressions were based on Pat O'Brien's wife in the movie. Quirk smiled knowledgeably.

"We're lucky she didn't have him buried where the plane crashed. Or take the body back to Chicago."

"Kansas! Chicago!"

Bramble took these possibilities as Father Quirk's namesake might take two more arrows. He shuddered and closed his eyes. He opened them on his renewed resolution.

"I want Rockne buried on campus."

"You'll have to get the family's permission."

"Why would they object?"

"Who makes up the family?" Roger asked.

Father Quirk might keep the flame of Rockne lighted, but his devotion was not transferable to the family, heirs, and progeny of the magnificent Norwegian.

"I'll look it up," Roger promised Bramble.

"What do you think of my idea?"

"A sarcophagus?"

Bramble looked to the others for help.

"Where would you relocate the grave, Father Quirk?"

"I'd leave it where it is." A grin spread slowly over the parchment skin. "Leave all rocks unturned."

*   *   *

Even outside in Bramble's car the sound of Quirk's cackling laughter as Father Carmody wheeled the old priest off to his room where he planned to watch the Bears game seemed to linger.

"He doesn't like the idea," Bramble said morosely.

"He may be thinking of opposition from the family."

"Maybe you could do something at Highland Cemetery."

Bramble shook his head. "No. I want to do something on campus."

That 'something' seemed to loosen up the situation, permitting his resolution to remain firm, but its implementation open to redefinition.

"A museum might be nice," Roger murmured.

"A museum!"

"The exhibits in the Joyce Center are nice. And there is a good special collection on sports in the library. There must be other paraphernalia of the Rockne era scattered around. I am told that the F. X. Bourke papers and memorabilia will come to the university. Bring all that together in a tasteful setting, a building centrally located. . . ."

Bramble clapped his hands and his eyes were aglow. "That is a terrific idea, Professor Knight!"

Roger smiled. He was thinking of an exhibit of Rockne's novel. Was there perhaps a manuscript, page proofs, a record of the stages through which the story had passed from original idea to finished book?

"Keep talking, Professor, please."

Roger talked all the way back to the apartment. He promised to draw up a prospectus of the idea for Bramble.

"And send it direct to me, not to the administration."

"I'll need your address."

Clearly Bramble felt that he had more than accomplished the purpose that had been formed ad hoc when Roger suggested he attend Mass at Holy Cross House. He had resumed something of his normal manner when they drew up at the apartment.

"Did your brother have an enjoyable dinner with Madeline?"

"I think he did."

"This may deflate him, Professor Knight, but I can't hold it back. After the lady dropped your brother off, she came by the

Morris Inn for a nightcap. I happened to be in the bar. We closed it, I'll tell you that. What a lady."

"Was she still opposed to your Rockne memorial?"

"We talked of other things." He looked at his watch. "I invited her to fly to Detroit for the game this afternoon."

"Then you haven't heard?"

Bramble just looked at Roger.

"Heard what?"

"She was found dead at her home this morning."

Bramble's mouth dropped open. He began slowly to shake his head.

"Dead? Why, she was a young woman." Then he paid deference to the awesomeness of death. "We just never know, do we? She did drink like a fish, though."

"She was killed."

Bramble's brow darkened. "I'll bet I know who did it."

"Her husband?"

Bramble shook his head impatiently. "Some guy named Hadley. He was stalking her, she said. I took her to her door because of that."

10

A meeting was in progress in the main building at Notre Dame, convened by Lincoln Logan, Vice-President of Public Relations, to examine the impact on the university of the death of one of its trustees. And more than a trustee. Madeline Rune's family connection to Notre Dame extended back several generations and there was every reason to fear that the unscrupulous media might maliciously use this tragic event to besmirch the reputation of the premier Catholic university in the land.

"The story hasn't broken nationally yet," Mario Miranda, university counsel, said.

"It was on WBBM an hour ago."

"What did they say?"

"That Stanley Rune's wife had been found dead in their country home."

"I talked with Mayor Barry," Miranda said.

The university counsel was a spidery man with an olive-shaped head on which it was difficult to believe that hair had ever grown. He was a graduate of Creighton in Omaha but three years in the Notre Dame Law School had removed this stain from his soul and turned him into a two hundred percent loyalist. Seven years of private practice and inspired investing had brought him back to South Bend a wealthy man, eager to serve his alma mater pro bono. He had required no instructions to go immediately into action when Myrtle nudged him awake so he could hear the local news report about the death of Madeline Rune. Myrtle was if anything more sensitive than Mario to the possible damage to the reputation of the university. Propped on his elbow, Mario listened to the halting reading of the item by a weekend substitute at the local station and alarms went off in his head. In the hours prior to the meeting in Lincoln's office, he had been busy about his alma mater's business.

"What's the problem?" Mayor Barry asked.

"The dead woman is Madeline Rune."

"Yeah?"

Miranda explained to the half-awake mayor that the dead woman was a trustee of the university, daughter of a family long connected with Notre Dame, and that it was a matter of great concern to the university that the investigation into Mrs. Rune's death be conducted in an efficient and professional manner.

"How'd you hear of it, Mario?"

"On the radio."

"What do you expect me to do?"

"Talk to the man in charge so that he fully understands the situation."

"I'll get in touch with Chief Polanski."

"You could instruct me to have a talk with him on your behalf."

There was a pause during which the mayor weighed the desirability of getting back to sleep against delegating his authority to the university's counsel. As an elected official he did not want to lay himself open to a charge of giving special consideration to the area's largest employer. On the other hand, he was conscious of the deference shown him in assigning a dozen seats at home games for his distribution. The issue was clear even to his sleep-drugged mind. Was he the servant of the people or the creature of the University of Notre Dame?

"Sure, Mario. Go ahead."

"You talk to the mayor?" Polanski asked when Miranda met with him.

"He sent me to you."

Polanski nodded. His off-duty officers earned welcome extra income directing game-time traffic for the university and Po-lanski himself had a seat in the press box.

"I've put Waring in charge of the inves-tigation."

"Waring." It was a question. Polanski hesitated.

"Purdue. But a good cop."

"What exactly happened to Madeline Rune?"

"She got killed."

"That for sure?"

Polanski thought about it. A natural death obviously had its attractions for Mario. In case he hadn't got that, Miranda began to sketch the send-off the university would like to give its late trustee. That her life had ended only hours after the initial triumph of the year in Notre Dame stadium was a fact with which the homilist could go to town. Miranda grew solemn as he described the obsequies for Madeline Rune. Clearly it would be a shame to tarnish such a magnificent ceremony with talk of violence, to say nothing of manslaughter.

The chief of police got the point. If it was impossible to obtain a verdict of natural death, he was to do all he could to bring the least serious charge.

"We may not even find out who did it," Polanski murmured.

Miranda did not smile. The string of unsolved and thus unprosecuted local murders had achieved the dimensions of a scandal. It occurred to him that if he had to bet whether Polanski's department would identify Madeline Rune's killer he would not risk a large sum of money.

Miranda decided that the body should be claimed by the university, and he telephoned Coffert the undertaker to tell him that he would be in charge of Madeline Rune's funeral.

"She writing her will?"

"It's already written."

"She ill?"

"She's dead."

"I hadn't heard." There was a note of self-reproach in Coffert's voice. It did not behoove an undertaker to be unaware of those who had left this world—or of the mortal coil they had shuffled off and left behind.

"Where's the body?"

"In the morgue. Tell them the body is to be released to Notre Dame. For an official funeral."

"There'll have to be an autopsy."

Miranda took a deep breath. His expression was that of a practiced lawyer trying to remember the tones of one telling the truth.

"Alex," he began, and stopped, remembering that Coffert's name was Albert. "Al, there aren't many people I could speak to as I can to you. You and I know what the family of Madeline Rune has meant to this community."

"And to Notre Dame."

"Few things are more dispiriting than to see a person who was noble in life demeaned in death by becoming the object of sensational curiosity."

"You think she killed herself?" Polanksi seemed in search of a defensible reason for Miranda's suggestion.

The university counsel's eyes shone with speculation. "Even if that were the case, and understand I am neither confirming nor denying it, you and I would want to see a veil of discretion drawn over that fact. What is to be gained by subjecting her to degrading publicity?"

"She and her husband had separated, I understand."

"Call Crispin," Miranda advised and hung up. Crispin was the coroner. He was not confident that the potential damage to the university was under control.

"We mustn't exaggerate the negatives," Logan said some hours later, looking around at the little group gathered in his office.

Miranda said nothing. As a hobby, Lincoln Logan wrote oped columns for the local paper, most of them reminiscences of a dull childhood in southern Ohio. Some were titled "Thoughts While Shampooing." This invited and frequently received from readers the suggestion that he shave his head. Logan had called this meeting in a panic and now wanted to suggest that others were losing their cool.

"Maybe you should start to play up the Rockne memorial Bramble proposes."

Logan looked pained by the suggestion. His own instinct would have been to play the Marcus Bramble gift for all it was worth. Turning the public's attention to the memory of Knute Rockne was surefire positive publicity for the university. Unfortunately, Logan had been instructed to do absolutely nothing to disseminate the story. The powers that be had decided that benign neglect of the athletic tradition of the school was the path to excellence. Neglect had little effect in this instance, however, since Bramble was tooting his own horn from coast to coast. Logan felt that his thunder was being stolen, so he liked Miranda's suggestion and would pass it on to the higher-ups—as a thought of his own, of course.

Bramble's ten million dollars might yet be seen as an unequivocal boon to the University of Notre Dame.

11

Stanley Rune telephoned Chief Polanski at ten-seventeen that Sunday morning, demanding to know what had happened to his wife.

"Where are you calling from?"

"What the hell difference does that make?"

"I'd rather tell you this in person."

"She's dead, isn't she?" All the anger was gone from his voice. "I'm in Chicago."

"How long will it take you to get here?"

It was before noon when Rune entered Polanski's office. He came to a stop before the chief's desk, impeccably dressed, not a hair out of place, in good shape, no flush of exertion on the smooth skin of his face. In the meantime Polanski verified that Rune had been in town for the game yesterday.

"When did you go back to Chicago?"

Rune ignored that. "Tell me what happened to my wife."

He listened intently as Polanski summarized what they knew, or thought they knew, of the death of Madeline Rune.

"She was found on the porch?"

"By the guy who delivers the Sunday morning paper."

"You check him out?"

"Your wife had been dead several hours before the newspaper man got there."

"Man?"

"That's right." Someone had taken notes on how Scheuer had gotten into the newspaper delivery business, but Polanski didn't think Rune needed to hear that.

"How do you know when he got there, aside from what he says?"

"His wife was with him." Polanski paused. "Any other suggestions?"

"Now look here, Chief. . . ."

"Why don't you just listen to what you came here for. Then I want to ask you some questions."

Rune put his back to the back of his chair and looked at Polanski with contempt. "Like when I went back to Chicago?"

"Like who you went to the game with, what you did afterward, that sort of thing. You want to hear more about your wife?"

Rune could not know that he had been the object of Casimir Polanski's envious contempt for years. Polanski had been a great athlete in high school, halfback for St. Joseph's when they went all the way to the semifinals. As a kid growing up in South Bend, he had of course taken Notre Dame as the ideal of college sports. He had attended more basketball and football and hockey games than the most fanatic undergraduate possibly could have during a four-year stay. His dream had been to play in the stadium he knew as well as his backyard, but his classroom performance had not matched his athletic prowess. His application for admission to Notre Dame had been turned down. He went to the athletic department and talked to an assistant coach, trying to persuade him to put in a word for him.

"It doesn't work that way, Casimir."

"But I have a C+ average."

"It's not just grades."

Casimir got out the newspaper clippings that recorded his athletic feats. The coach nodded.

"We looked at you, Casimir."

His breath caught. Notre Dame coaches had actually scouted him? He waited. The coach looked away, then looked back.

"You're strong but you're not fast."

Fast like Stanley Rune was the way Polanski completed the thought that fall when he hung around practice, watching the group he might have been a part of. Rune started as a freshman, playing Casimir's position. He was not strong, but he was fast. Polanski developed the idea that Rune had stolen his spot on the team, that the career that brought Rune national attention had been meant for him. But for all his accomplishments at Notre Dame, Rune had not been drafted by the pros.

"Fast but not strong enough," a spokesman for the Bears said. The Bears were thought to have a moral obligation to sign every Notre Dame star.

Rune had married into the legendary local Bourke family, practiced law in Chicago, and all but commuted back and forth between South Bend and the city. The breakup of Stanley and Madeline had hit Notre Dame the way the dissolution of the House of Windsor had hit Great Britain. The unthinkable had happened. A Catholic couple separated, talked divorce, and there was no hope of an annulment. Madeline went on being a half-hearted flirt, escorted by a series of men, while Stanley made a fool of himself with younger women.

With a very much younger woman in the case of Pamela Menucci, the girl Stanley had taken to the game yesterday.

12

Luigi Menucci taught Italian, a language he had spoken since he was a child, but he felt like an impostor facing a classful of undergraduates, most of them with Italian names, wanting to learn the language of their forefathers—until they realized it took effort. That was when they began to blame their failure to learn on Menucci. He half agreed with them. Once he had drilled his students from a book, writing furiously on the board, saying the words or sentence and having them repeat them after him.

"This isn't high school," Fred Bass had said to him years ago. The German instructor had been lurking in the hallway of O'Shaughnessy, kibitzing on Menucci's Italian class. "You are a teacher, not a language coach."

I'm neither. He almost said it aloud. No criticism could be as severe as that he leveled at himself. Bass didn't have to mention that Menucci had no doctorate; that was conveyed in his tone of voice. He had been taken on by Father Rooney, who had known Menucci's parents. The whole family thought it was a blessing just fallen from the sky. Eventually Menucci realized he had been a bargain, and he still was. How could he argue for a raise when he didn't feel that he deserved what he was already being paid? It was worse when his daughter Pamela became an undergraduate. She was bright and confident and beautiful with her thick honey-blond hair and large brown eyes with brows that arced in constant delighted surprise. She wanted to be an architect.

"That's a five-year program."

"I can spend a year in Rome."

Of course she knew more about it than he did. Architecture was housed in what had once been the library in a time before

Menucci had been on the faculty. It was far off on the edge of campus; he almost never saw her except when she wanted to use the car, but he was aware of her presence always. His teaching grew worse. Bass was no longer there to comment, but he might just as well have been. Memory of the German professor lingered like a bad conscience. Of course language instruction had been transformed by all the electronic aids now available. Kids sat in language labs with earphones clamped to their heads listening to the language as taped by actors, to recorded newscasts from RAI 1, to drama, even opera. Menucci felt more superfluous than ever.

He was a thin, hawk-faced man whose still-thick hair had gone from black to silver between his thirty-eighth and fortieth years. Just like that. Once he heard a girl student saying how handsome he was. Of course he didn't believe it. He was a standard southern Italian type. Rune was medium-sized, balding, nothing to look at except for the smile. The first time he saw Pamela with him he hadn't suspected a thing. It was a conversation with Helmut Horst, Bass's successor, that prompted the suspicion—

no, the realization. The fleeting glimpse he had had of his daughter and the older man now was unmistakable.

"Parents should not have to worry that their children are prey to professors."

Menucci agreed, not getting the drift. Horst began a recital of incidents. They were all new to Menucci. Horst insisted that these were simply facts. Uncontested facts. His account made it sound as if the faculty were bent on seducing the student body.

"Your daughter's in architecture, isn't she?"

He welcomed the apparent change of subject. "Yes, yes. She loves it."

"I didn't know you drove a Porsche."

"I don't."

"I'm certain I've seen her in a Porsche."

Menucci drove a Toyota. He wanted to convey to Horst how proud he was of his daughter. Her success seemed to make up for his own career.

"Of course the man was driving."

"What man?"

"The man in the Porsche."

A less persistent gossip would have dropped it, but Horst went on relentlessly until Menucci grasped the incredible point.

Horst was telling him that he had seen Pamela in a Porsche with an older man several times. More than several times. A lot.

Of course Menucci dismissed these suspicions, even as all his own doubts fled. He too had seen Pamela with the man. He had assumed he was an instructor in architecture. It appeared that Horst thought so too. But Menucci learned who Rune was.

Spying on his own daughter, he felt worse than the man in whose company she constantly was.

13

Seven miles north of South Bend is Niles, Michigan, the town where Ring Lardner was raised, began his journalistic career, wooed and married a girl from Elkhart, and then left the region never to return. The Lardner house is on Main Street, but it is occupied, lived in, not a museum, and the interested tourist can only stare at it and then pass on.

Philip Knight had made discreet inquiries and had driven to Niles to see the horse farm on which Henry Hadley lived. Hadley, he had learned, was the last of a long South Bend line. His parents had been in

on Associates Investors when the shrewd
E. M. Morris had formed it during the thirties. People spoke in awed tones of how a
modest investment in Associates had
grown in a matter of years to a fortune, a
fortune that in turn pullulated in the vaults
of Associates until Croesus himself might
have envied the first generation of investors. Hadley had been a pharmacist when
he made his fortunate investment. Within a
year he had sold out and neither he nor any
of his kind had ever worked again.

Until Henry, that is, if you can call teaching work. He held a degree from IUSB and
had been taken on by the English Department at Notre Dame, because, Philip was
told, the university hoped that this lowering
of the standards would begin a flow of
money from the Hadley Foundation, a
source hitherto closed to Notre Dame and
immune to the blandishments of fund-
raisers.

Madeline Rune had been nearly twenty
years older than Hadley, but the young man
had conceived a passion for her that was
only fueled by her laughing dismissal of his
overtures. Interest on her part might have
stifled his ardor, but indifference coupled

with mocking laughter turned the older woman into a prize he was resolved to have. He had been reported to the police by Madeline.

"What could we do?" Waring said to Phil.

"Arrest him?"

"Not likely. His family has a far greater claim on local loyalty than hers. She understood that but refused to accept it. She was talking about hiring a private detective."

In Niles, Phil went up the steps to a porch which ran across the front of the house and continued around the corner. He had heard the chimes when he pressed the bell, three times and going on four, when he detected some movement behind the lace curtain of the glass door. Someone seemed to be watching him. He tried to strike an air that was meant to express his indifference to whether anyone answered the door. But he cared a lot. He pressed the bell again and there was a lacy movement and then the door handle began to turn.

"No one's home," an old lady said, looking out over the sturdy chain that permitted the door to open only a few inches.

"Mrs. Hadley?"

"Miss."

"Imogene Hadley!" The family sketch he had gotten from Waring had seemed useless information at the time. Now, knowing the name of the unmarried aunt proved an open sesame.

"Do I know you?"

"I doubt that you'll remember me."

Unfair, misleading, manipulative. But effective. The door closed and the chain clanked free like a sound effect in Dickens's *Christmas Carol*.

She seemed even shorter because she was bent over. Gray hair was pulled back from her face, emphasizing the noble nose. Great pouched eyes looked up at him, ready to spark with recognition.

"Actually, it was Caroline I knew."

He had been informed that there had been two unmarried sisters, of whom Imogene was the only survivor. The wide mouth turned down and deep lines appeared.

"Caroline has passed away."

They stood there, two strangers, talking about another stranger so far as Phil was concerned. He let out a great sigh and said if he didn't get off his feet he was going to collapse. Imogene too had an urge to sit. She led him back into the kitchen where there was coffee on the stove.

"Where did you meet Caroline?"

He found that he could no longer go on with the charade, not sitting here at her kitchen table drinking her coffee. He took a card from his wallet and pushed it across the table to her. She held it close to her face for a moment and then looked over it at him.

"I can't read it."

"It says I am a detective."

It was her turn to sigh. "I was sure you were another one."

"It's important for us to talk to the family at a time like this."

"Madeline Rune." She shook her head. "Do you know, I didn't even know who they were talking about."

"You don't know her?"

"Not really. The family, of course. Whose daughter is she, exactly?"

"Henry was very devoted to her."

"That's what they told me. It was the first I heard of it. They must be mistaken. They said she was fifty years old."

Rounding it off. She had been forty-nine.

Phil said that was still young to die. She looked alarmed. The thought of death was obviously not one she wished to become familiar with. Phil checked a little surge of condescension. Would he be any less fearful of death when he was her age? If he ever reached her age.

"Your nephew lives here with you?"

"I am the one who lives with him. I represent the poor relations. This house and all the rest is his."

"All the rest?"

"It is common knowledge that Henry came into a fortune when he turned twenty-one. He let Caroline and me stay on here. It is the only place we ever lived."

"Was he here last night?"

"Why don't you ask me the questions?" Phil turned to see a rumpled young man standing in the doorway. His jogging suit was soggy with sweat and so was the band around his head.

"This is another detective," Imogene said.

"How many of you people are going to come here bothering my aunt?"

"Could we talk?"

"I'm going to take a shower."

"I'll wait."

Hadley glared at him and then thundered down the basement steps.

"He went down."

"His apartment is down there. He is a very private person."

"He can come and go without bothering you?"

"He wouldn't bother me."

After a few minutes, Philip rose and told Imogene he would go downstairs to talk with Henry. She nodded resignedly. The steps creaked beneath him, but as he descended he heard a shower running. He was surprised by the Spartan circumstances of Henry Hadley's quarters. He had just been told that Henry was heir to a fortune, yet the makeshift apartment in the basement of the mansion made the places where graduate students lived look good. The shower was an enclosed cabinet that had been put up near a floor drain: it looked like one of the portable toilets set in rows on the edges of parking lots at home games. The little cabinet reverberated with the sound of rushing water. A trail of discarded jogging clothes led from a door that opened into the apartment. Once more austerity was the keynote: there was a large, flat table on which a computer and printer stood. The swivel chair facing the keyboard was little more than a stool with back support. The computer was on and there was a Picasso screen saver, the *Demoiselles of Avignon*. Philip touched the space bar and a title page came into view. *The Four Losers—the students, the alumni, the faculty, and the faith. College Football at the End of the Millennium*, by Henry Hadley.

"You can read it when it's published," Hadley said behind him.

Phil did not turn but scrolled down to where the text began.

On month, day, year in Lansing, Michigan, the Notre Dame football program took a fateful turn. Ranked Number 1 in the nation going into the game, Notre Dame found itself in a struggle for its life. With the score tied at 10-10, Ara Parseghian faced a decision that proved to be a turning point. Late in the fourth quarter, in possession of the ball, Notre Dame had the opportunity to go for a victory or to play out the clock and secure a tie and the national championship. Notre Dame chose to tie. The national championship was clinched, but in the process a program that had been predicated on the building of character, the pursuit of excellence, victory, became a means of achieving a ranking. . . .

"Not a bad beginning." Phil turned just in time to sidestep the baseball bat that Hadley was swinging at him. He grabbed the barrel of the bat to deflect it and twisting it to one side sent Hadley toppling to the floor. The bat rolled free. Phil snatched it up and stood over the fallen Hadley. It was tempting to give him a taste of that bat, but Phil was elated by his near escape. He examined the bat.

"A Louisville Slugger."

"It was used by Mickey Mantle."

"He wouldn't have missed."

"He struck out a lot." Hadley got to his feet and backed away from Phil. "Now get the hell out of my room."

"Where were you last night?"

Hadley tried surprise, then laughed. "I had a date with a graduate student named

Katherine George. We were at a postgame party off campus."

"Madeline Rune told people that you had been bothering her, Hadley. You're sure you weren't stalking her Saturday night?"

Hadley laughed again. "Ah, the delusions of the older woman. Anyway, you can check with my girl."

"Katherine George."

"I understand that you had dinner with Madeline Saturday night."

14

In the university club, waitresses caucused
from time to time in the little room called,
for reasons lost in the mists of the past, the
Library. It was devoid of books and, today,
of diners. Here, on their way to and from
the kitchen and the main dining area, waitresses could exchange information on what
their tables were saying about the news of
the day.

"They don't know anything."

"They're talking about her family."

"The husband killed her."

"She had a boyfriend."

"Boy's the word too."

"When isn't it?"

They dispersed, giggling, a momentary congregation of birds, flying off in different directions, but returning again and again to exchange more telegraphic communications.

"The lawyers say the husband."

"The locker room"—for such was their derisive label for those who called themselves the jock table—"says she was with someone else Saturday night."

"My sister saw them at the Carriage House."

"The Carriage House!"

"She works there."

Relief. "The Old Bastards claim she had a late date."

Various Midwestern versions of what was once known as the Bronx cheer signaled another breakup of the group.

"My nephew told me," assistant dean Waddick said with finality. Waddick *locutus est, causa finita est.*"

"Waddick the dick?"

"He's my wife's nephew."

This relative, now characterized as shirttail, was a clerk at police headquarters and had heard of the late-night get together of Bramble and Madeline Rune.

"A last-minute substitute."

"The guy she had dinner with is the brother of Roger Knight."

"The Goodyear blimp?"

The emeriti fell silent, reflecting on the alleged facts swirling about the violent death of Madeline Rune. These scholars had never taken part in the home game frolics the administration put on for trustees and donors who were in town for the weekend. On Thursdays and Fridays before home games, the private planes began to arrive— corporate jets, family craft, rented wings, the affluent dropping in for the weekend. Stretch limos came along the interstate from Chicago and others from the East, converging on the campus and stadium and the planned and unplanned celebrating. The Morris Inn housed the *crème de la crème* as well as those whose claim on rooms was hereditary, much as was their claim on tickets to the game. In some cases, the second and third generations of earlier movers and shakers had descended the economic scale and moved with resentful defiance among the affluent in the lobby of the Inn, filling the main dining room and all the auxiliary rooms where special class dinners were held, as well as packing the bar. Across the street at the equivocally named Center for Continuing Education on all floors cocktail parties and catered meals began on Friday night and resumed on Saturday after the game. At such fetes might be seen legends of commerce and industry as well as of entertainment. The highest echelons of the American hierarchy, both political and ecclesiastical, were represented. All this was remote from the lives of those at the Old Bastards table and they spoke of the shenanigans of these migrants as natives of Pacific atolls might speculate about the great silver birds that left contrails in the sky as they passed mysteriously overhead.

To one of these gatherings the soon-to-be-slain trustee had gone, then off she went to dinner with the aforementioned Philip Knight; afterward she had dropped him off at his apartment and then apparently stopped at the Morris Inn to continue drinking with the redoubtable Bramble.

*   *   *

"Bramble apparently saw her last," an authoritative voice at the law table said.

"Last?"

"Penultimately," came the cautious correction.

It was observed that there were enough sides to the situation for bridge. The victim, God rest her soul, her husband, an infatuated younger man, and a late night rendezvous with the nut who wanted to resurrect Rockne and scatter his ashes over the field at the next contest with USC.

This last was ruled out of order as malicious and unfounded speculation, but the four protagonists survived subsequent cross and recross.

"They're separated?"

"He's going through a midlife crisis."

"At his age?" The speaker, suited, bobbed hair, was still in her twenties, a visitor for the semester from her position at Justice in Washington. The question was deemed an unseemly reference to her age and precocity and passed over in silence.

"A faculty child."

"Child?"

"Daughter of Menucci who teaches Italian."

* * *

Bob Leader returned the little bottle containing the remainder of his executive martini to its bed of ice after replenishing his glass and said to Otto Bird, "All this would have been unthinkable only a few years ago."

"All what?"

But a gesture sufficed. The two emeriti were of one mind in their estimation of the direction the university had gone. Bird had been the founder and first director of the General Program of Liberal Education; Leader painted and designed stained-glass and for decades had taught a legendary course in art history. It was not a dozen years since they had retired. Once a week they shared a prolonged lunch in the University Club where, fortified by executive martinis and then burgundy with the meal, they were able to derive some satisfaction from their dissatisfaction with the modern world.

"I am reading Waugh," Bird said.

"Which one?"

"Evelyn."

Leader frowned. The waitress came and checked the level of the iced bottles.

Leader nodded and she went off for replacements.

"I'm thinking of giving a million dollars to bury Gerry Faust."

"Is he dead?"

"From the neck up."

It was an old grievance, five years of football failure under the reign of Faust.

"He must have sold his soul to the devil."

"The devil's no fool."

"Ho ho," Bird said appreciatively, and two more executive martinis arrived in what Leader called specimen bottles. At the jock table, interest in the violent death of Madeline Rune had subsided and the conversation had returned to replaying last Saturday's game.

"The tight end. Why doesn't he throw to the tight end at least once or twice in the season."

"Once or twice on Saturday and we would have gotten another fourteen points. He was wide open. . . ."

But the offensive line, a favorite topic, was raised and the diners huddled forward. Here was a problem a man could get his teeth into.

"They can't block."

"He's the fat professor with the good-looking brother," a voice among the momentarily assembled waitresses said.

"They say he's brilliant."

"The brother?"

"Fatso."

"I've never seen him."

"Because you only work lunches. They come in the evening, with the townies."

Membership in the University Club was open to citizens of South Bend and beyond, part of the continuing effort to promote good relations between town and gown. As the largest employer in the area, Notre Dame enjoyed an equivocal status, some proletarian resentment of the lord of the manor, but on the whole an esteem and loyalty wholly incommensurate with the unadorned facts. For those who joined, dining at the club was a welcome alternative to area restaurants.

"The brother eats as much as he does."

"Which brother?"

"Either one. They both really put it away."

15

When Marcus Bramble called to say that
the more he thought of it the more he liked
the idea of a museum, Roger did not at first
know what the generous alumnus was talking about.

"What's a grave going to do for the campus?" Bramble said. "What did that priest
call it, a soccerfogus?"

"A sarcophagus."

"Yeah. Anyway, a Rockne museum is a
great idea. Where do you think it should
go?"

"That's hardly for me to say."

"Sure it is. Let's talk, decide where it should go, and I'll write it into the gift."

"You could have the architecture school put students on it as a project. A prize for the best design."

Bramble liked that almost as much as he had liked the idea for a museum. He came by to take Roger to lunch at the Morris Inn and led him in as if he were a free agent he had just signed for one of his teams. They had a table in the lower portion of the dining room, near a window looking out at a putting green that appeared forlorn now that the golf course beyond was being built on and was destined to become merely an extension of the campus.

"I loved that golf course," Bramble said, shaking his head. "That's what bothers me about these new guys. No sense of the past. You know, I think they're half embarrassed by the mention of Knute Rockne."

"That's hard to believe."

"Isn't it?"

A vice-president stopped by their table, spoke unctuously to Bramble and glanced warily at Roger.

"What are you two conspiring?"

"You'll be the first to know, Father."

"Promise?" But he punched Bramble lightly on the arm before going off to the corner high table that since Father Hesburgh had been the designated table of the high administration. Bramble leaned toward Roger.

"You thought about what would go in the museum?"

Roger gave Bramble a brief account of what, with the aid of Greg Whelan, he had learned of the archives holdings. Greg was certain that collateral holdings, not listed in Unloc, would yield a good deal more.

"Rockne has not been a high priority," the archivist explained. "Not enough scholarly interest."

Breathless books by logorrheic sportswriters appeared regularly, of course, but they just recycled the same material. A few years ago, a graduate student had begun a debunking series in the *Observer*, but that effort had ended abruptly.

"He was denied further access," Whelan said, his tone even.

"Who was it?"

"Our friend Hadley. He was a student then."

Hadley's iconoclastic impulses had been diverted at the time to a skeptical account of Dr. Tom Dooley, the doctor who had worked himself to death in Laos and been effectively canonized by Father Hesburgh. A statue of Dooley, who had died a very young man, now stood near the grotto, itself a replica of the grotto of Lourdes.

Hadley had made irreverent references to Father Sorin's devotion to Bernadette and Lourdes and it was these, rather than his attempt to demythologize Dooley, that had drawn attention. In what might have been a tongue-in-cheek letter to the editor, Hadley vowed that he would say a rosary at the grotto every day for a month asking for forgiveness for any offense he had given.

Bramble observed that the university had paid more attention to Dooley than to Rockne.

"He wasn't even an alumnus. There's a shrine to him in the student center!"

Roger wondered how many would share Bramble's belief that Notre Dame ignored or downplayed its greatest coach. A case could be made that few press releases about football or Notre Dame athletics in general failed to allude at least to the legendary coach. And of course the movie was shown as part of orientation to each entering class. A columnist in the *Observer* had interpreted Bramble's gift as a plan to replace the Lady on the golden dome with Knute Rockne.

"Kids," Bramble said, shaking his head.

Actually the author was a junior member of the Government department.

Bramble was visibly disappointed with what Roger had so far turned up from the archives. Letters, clippings, academic records, contracts—none of these had struck the enthusiastic alumnus as having the power to touch off the proper excitement and devotion in the students of the future. He fell silent and Roger wondered if the thought of a great mausoleum in the center of campus was not once more exerting its old attraction on Bramble.

"What was that book you mentioned?"

"Rockne's novel?"

Bramble nodded. "Where can I get a copy?"

"That may be possible. I'm told it was reprinted by a local publisher a few years ago."

"How'd he get permission?"

"It's in the public domain."

"Didn't anyone renew the copyright?"

This reinforced his view that the university was unappreciative of Knute Rockne. On the other hand, Bramble's interest in the novel had dimmed and he seemed to regard it as on a par with the unexciting items in the archives. Roger decided against trying to convince Bramble otherwise. He was finding the man too volatile. The mention of the possibility of a museum had not been the expression of any deep desire on Roger's part. As for himself, he was content to pursue the spoor of the novel. Carmody arranged for him to spend a few hours with old Father Quirk, recording what the old man remembered. He did not of course mention to Bramble his own sense of an inadequate urgency in recording the memories of such ancients as Father Quirk. All too soon, alas, their memories would go with them to the grave.

"What sort of reception did the novel receive, Father Quirk?"

"Not much. He wasn't a legend then, you know; he was just the football coach. If Lou

Holtz wrote a book would the world stop spinning?"

"I think he did."

Father Quirk opened his hands in a QED.

"Was Rockne disappointed?"

Quirk shook his head. "Being a novelist was not one of his ambitions. His other projects looked more promising to him and he devoted most of his attention to them."

"What was your job exactly?"

Father Quirk moved a colorless tongue along his lower lip, but both tongue and lip were dry. "I typed up the written manuscript."

"That typescript is in the archives."

"Have you seen it?"

"Yes."

The pale eyes seemed to focus on some distant object. "It's strange to think of that still in existence."

"It will outlast us both."

"It will certainly outlast me."

"What happened to the manuscript."

"Isn't it there?"

"There's no record of it."

"Good."

"Why do you say that?"

"It was a mess."

"Rockne's handwriting looks pretty legible to me. On other things."

Father Quirk thought about that. "I meant it was disorganized."

Greg Whelan was making inquiries of the heirs of the original publishers, to see what sales data might be available. Newspaper and periodical checks had not turned up much by way of reviews until Whelan turned to the university's own sports collection. The sports world had been amused by Rockne's foray into literature. A recurrent judgment was that he was no Ring Lardner.

"There seems to have been little local notice."

"You mean the *Scholastic*? They were always light on sports news."

Father Quirk's account of exactly how he had worked with Rockne on the novel was alternately precise and vague. Did he get chapters as they were finished or was he given the whole manuscript?

"I didn't start typing before I had the whole."

"Did you get it all at once?"

Quirk was not sure. Did he type it in his room? Most of it had been done in the room on the third floor of the main building where

copies of the novel had been found long
after it had been forgotten. One of the sup-
ports of the dome ran through a corner of
the office and into it the walk-in safe had
been embedded. It was in there that pack-
ages of the novel had been discovered in
the 1950s, wrapped in plain paper.

"Why did the athletic office need a safe?"

"The safe was there when Rock was
given the office. I think the treasurer had
occupied it before."

This created the image of far simpler or-
ganization than the university had now.
Considering the stature Rockne had ac-
quired posthumously, the thought of him
being put into an office that had been vacated by a university officer suggested a
charming informality.

"He must have stored those copies of the
book in the safe."

"I suppose."

Roger found that he was disappointed
with the contemporary reaction Quirk suggested. When Roger had found a copy of
the novel in a used bookstore in Yonkers
he had been delighted. It had seemed to
recall a forgotten flurry of excitement and at
least fleeting fame, but Quirk would have

him believe that the novel had meant little to Rockne, had created no sensation, and had at most provided sportswriters with an opportunity to condescend to a coach who had invaded what they probably thought of as their domain.

"I wouldn't make too much of it, Professor."

"It fascinates me."

"That is because you are a professor. The past always looks more interesting than the present to scholars."

"I am hardly a scholar, Father Quirk."

"And Knute Rockne was hardly a novelist."

16

The autopsy report obviously did not please Miranda, who had accompanied Phil to the county morgue. He suggested that it had been precipitous to conclude that Madeline Rune had been killed.

"Do you think it was an accident?"

"She had been drinking. She could have tripped."

"Wasn't there a head wound?"

Miranda seemed not to hear. "And she had a weak heart."

It seemed clear that Miranda was expressing his hopes rather than a viable interpretation of the facts. Weir, the assistant coroner, announced that death had been caused by the delivery of a severe blow to the back of the head.

"While she was still in the house. Or on her way out. The door was open and she fell through it onto the floor of the porch."

Miranda asked if the wound on the back of the head could have been caused by the deceased banging into something.

"Say she lost her balance inside the house, spun, fell back against the frame of the door, and then collapsed onto the floor porch."

"That's very unlikely."

"Did you check it out?"

Waring said that the police report mentioned no evidence on the door frame to support the hypothesis.

"Was the door frame examined?"

"Nothing was noticed."

"That's obvious. I think Dr. Weir should delay release of his report until there has been a more thorough examination of the scene of Mrs. Rune's death. We don't want to go chasing after an assassin if what we have here is a tipsy woman suffering a fatal blow in a fall."

Weir wrinkled his nose as he consulted

his report. "It's possible that the wound could have been caused by the sharp edge of a doorframe."

Miranda got the delay he wanted, although why he wanted it Phil could not understand. Pictures of the death scene supported the explanation with which Weir had begun. But when the university attorney was told that the body could not be released until his alternative theory had been checked out, he seemed ready to withdraw his hypothesis.

"The university wants to make plans for the funeral."

"This was your idea," Weir said petulantly.

"How long will it take?"

"Long enough so I don't have some other damn fool notions thrown at me when I make my next report."

"This is not a criticism of your professional competence."

"Of what then, my golf swing? Come on. You're saying the police overlooked the obvious and I don't know the difference between an ashtray and a doorframe."

"But you said it was possible."

"Everything is."

This metaphysical remark was allowed to dissolve in the resulting silence.

"What do you think?" Phil asked Waring.

"She got hit on the back of the head with something heavy and cheap."

"So why delay?"

Waring shrugged. "Let's go out to the house."

Phil and Waring went off with Crispin from the medical examiner's office. There was no blood on the doorframe.

"I could have told him that," said Crispin.

From the dining room window Phil looked out at the great four-stall garage and remembered that Madeline had said that a graduate student lived there. When Waring came to see if he was headed back to South Bend, Phil told him to go ahead. Waring hesitated but did not ask why Phil was staying.

"I wonder if Mrs. Taylor is home."

"Can't you hear?"

The faint roar of a television on the third floor was audible. Phil waved to Waring and started up the broad staircase to the upper floors, not looking back. The front door opened and closed, but he did not check to see if Waring had gone until he reached the landing. There was no sign of the South Bend detective in the foyer below.

Madeline's description of this house which she had both loved and hated had been so vivid that Phil felt he could draw a floorplan, at least of the second floor. He turned to the right and went down the wide, carpeted hallway toward the double doors at the end. When he turned the knob, he told himself the room would be locked, but the door opened. He opened both doors then and surveyed the workroom of F. X. Bourke. There was a large trestle table desk facing the double doors and behind it a huge bowed window which, Phil knew, looked out over the river.

"He always faced away from the river when he worked. He said that otherwise he would have done nothing but watch that slow mesmerizing movement of the St. Joe." Madeline had half-closed her eyes as she said this, and it had the sound of quotation. Bourke had been a master of the memorable phrase.

Below the window a low bookcase followed its curved contours. On a table at right angles to the desk stood the large typewriter on which Bourke had pounded out his columns and books. The sheer labor that writing had once been was symbolized by that mechanical typewriter. A great oval rag rug covered the floor in front of the desk. Phil moved to the center of it and then looked from left to right. A work table to the right was covered with irregular stacks of paper, magazines, and books, and to the left were shelves on which were displayed a sampling of the awards and trophies Bourke had been given over the years. Phil turned to look at the bookshelves that rose from floor to ceiling and where the once bright dust jackets of Bourke's personal library were faded with time. There were many volumes related to sports, but there were also the classics of which Bourke had been a great devotee, peppering his columns with allusions to the *Iliad* and the *Aeneid*, giving a tag of Horace in Latin as if his readers were as educated as he was. As he browsed along the shelves, Phil was surprised to come upon a series of boys books featuring one Lance

Urbansky, who seemed to have excelled in every sport. Phil took one from the shelf, *The Big Game*, and opened it.

Lance, he read, took the ball from the center and stepped back five yards as if to throw a pass and the line let the two Lawrenceville linebackers through. Just before Lance tossed the ball to his left, the huge Lawrenceville players crashed into him and he went down in a starburst of pain. Moments later when he was helped to his feet, he learned that Holt had caught the ball when he tossed it to him and then had sprinted thirty-five yards for a touchdown. There was half a minute left to play. Halton Academy had beaten Lawrenceville!

Phil closed the book and looked at the cover. The author was William X. McNaughton. McNaughton? He wished Madeline was still alive so he could ask her if her grandfather had written boys books under a pseudonym. How different this story was from the one Hadley was writing.

He went to the window and again looked out at the garage. From this angle he could see a light on. Had Mrs. Taylor told the police about the student living there?

He closed the double doors of the study

and went back to the staircase and paused, listening to the roar of television on the third floor. Mrs. Taylor was watching the Bears game. He decided not to bother her.

To find the entrance to the apartment he had to walk along the side of the garage to the back where a door opened onto a stairway that rose steeply to the upper level. Phil took the stairs two at a time and rapped on the door. A voice shouted for him to come in, but he waited until the door was opened from the inside. An attractive young woman looked out at him with both surprise and disappointment.

"Have the police talked with you yet?"

"The police!"

Was it possible that the commotion of that Sunday morning had not penetrated to the garage? When he came out of the house, Phil had stood in front of the closed doors of the garage and looked toward the house. The drive led away from the doors and then swept around the front of the house to join the great looping drive that came up from the country road and then returned to it.

"What's your name?" he asked the young woman.

"Katherine George. Are you a policeman?"

Phil got out his wallet and flashed his private investigator's license. But she reached out and took it. Her eyes lifted to his.

"Knight?"

"Philip Knight."

"I have a professor named Knight."

"Roger? He's my brother."

All wariness was gone now and she asked him in, chattering about what a wonderful person Roger was, and so intelligent! Phil was having difficulty putting this lovely girl together with Henry Hadley. The embittered assistant professor seemed to have made a religion out of avoiding barbers and shampoo, his clothes looked like rejects from St. Vincent de Paul, and whatever wonder and delight he had originally had at the prospects before him were long since gone. What attraction could he have for this bright and lovely girl?

"How well do you know your landlady?"

"Landlady?"

"Mrs. Rune."

"Oh, I have nothing to do with her. I rented the house from the Walkers."

"You don't know Madeline Rune?"

"Not really. I see her from time to time. She's living in the house now."

"Henry Hadley told me he had a post-game date with you Saturday."

Her expression changed. "Is this why you're asking me about Mrs. Rune?"

"What's the connection?"

"She has some silly notion that Henry is pursuing her. She is old enough to be his mother! If that's the reason you're here, you are being used by a foolish woman."

"Madeline Rune is dead."

"What?"

"Didn't you hear sirens Sunday morning? Don't you read the paper?" But of course Miranda had managed to get the story buried on page 14.

"What happened to her?"

"Someone killed her."

"Oh, my gosh."

"When did you get home Saturday night?"

"It was Sunday morning. After two. I slept until noon." She paused. "We went to Mass at Stepan Center after the game." Again she paused and then looked at him with widened eyes. "You don't think Henry had anything to do with. . . ."

"Did he bring you home?"

She nodded.

"What time was that?"

"He came in and stayed awhile. To talk."

"For how long."

"Not an hour." She looked at him anxiously. "When did Mrs. Rune die?"

"She was killed between three and four in the morning."

17

Waring came by for dinner and Roger made spaghetti while Philip tossed up a huge salad. The South Bend detective sat sipping Chianti, watching the two brothers.

"You two make batching it look attractive."

"You married?"

"I was."

A silence. It was the kind of answer that did not invite further questions.

"She died. Just like that, an aneurysm."

"How long ago?"

"April."

"This past April?"

Waring nodded. "I haven't eaten at home since."

Clearly it is one thing to have lost a wife and quite another never to have had one. Having mentioned his loss, Waring seemed almost to regret the confidence, but it made him a far more sympathetic character. Maybe he thought he owed them some kind of autobiography since he had quizzed them the first time they met. But he had been acting in an official capacity, investigating the Madeline Rune murder. They had gathered tonight to talk about what had been learned in the two days since the body was found. But not before they had eaten. Waring and Phil had wine with the meal and Roger, who never drank, had a Diet Pepsi. "Drinking a diet drink with pasta," he observed, "qualifies as a gustatory denial of the principle of contradiction." Neither Phil nor Waring commented on this. And then the dishes were in the dishwasher and the three men got comfortable in the living room of the small apartment. The Knight brothers looked receptively at Waring.

"From the beginning?"

"Of the investigation," Roger replied. "We will stipulate the Book of Genesis."

"On Sunday morning at or about five o'clock the body of Madeline Rune had been found on the porch of her family home by the man who delivered the Sunday papers. The paramedics pronounced her dead at the scene and had called in the medical examiner. The preliminary judgment that death had been caused by a blow to the back of the head had been borne out by Weir's report."

"Not due to falling against the doorframe," Roger suggested.

"Could it have been a baseball bat?" Phil asked.

"Why think so?"

"I'll tell you later."

Systematically they went through the investigation and at the end seemed to have come up with a number of people who could have killed Madeline.

"Her husband, obviously."

"Hadn't he returned to Chicago after the game?"

"He changed his story. After I found he had registered in a local motel."

"Meaning that he was in South Bend when Madeline was killed?"

Waring nodded. "And, of course, there is Phil here."

"You flatter me."

Waring went impassively on. "You take the lady to dinner, you are susceptible to her charms, and perhaps your amorous appetites are aroused, but she drops you off at your apartment. You stand, watching the car go off and then notice it pull into the Morris Inn drive. Madeline gets out and goes inside. Surprised, you cross the street and enter the inn. You see Madeline and Marcus Bramble in the bar together."

Phil just smiled. "So you have gotten to Marcus Bramble."

"Right. Earlier the lady had mocked his intention to endow a fitting memorial to Knute Rockne. He has been brooding over this put-down which, added to the lack of enthusiasm on the part of the administration, has made him surly. In the bar, Madeline takes up again her mocking dismissal of his heart's desire. He persuades her to let her driver go."

"A rental car?"

"Connell Livery. The rental ran until 11:50

Saturday night, which is when she told the driver that was all. Bramble had offered to take her home whenever she wanted to go. He did so and there did her in."

"Going inside first so she could fall outside."

"Maybe she asked him in."

"Anybody else?"

"Henry Hadley."

"Do you seriously give credence to the story that this young man was pursuing a woman the age of Madeline Rune?" Roger asked the question without any skepticism. He had long since learned to disclaim any understanding of what drew a man and woman together or of what subsequently could drive them apart. No generalizations worked. The reasons were as various as the occurrences. As hundreds of songwriters have said, love is a mystery.

"She filed an informal complaint."

"Informal."

"She spoke to Chief Polanski about it."

"Where was Hadley Saturday night?"

"At a postgame party on campus."

"For how long?"

"He's not sure. Until after midnight. When he went home to bed."

Phil intervened to tell of his interview with Katherine George and his encounter with Hadley at his home. "This is where the baseball bat comes in."

"The baseball bat?"

"The one he tried to hit me with. From behind. When I was prying into his personal affairs, namely a dreadful novel called *The Four Losers.*"

"His anti-Rockne novel," Roger said.

"The bat was a Louisville Slugger."

"You examined it?"

"I did."

"Was there any sign that it had been used as a murder weapon?"

"No. In any case, it suggests his way of dealing with troublesome matters. And he was there that night."

He told them what Katherine George had told him. Hadley had left her apartment before three, not long before the time of death established by Weir.

"And his motive is what, thwarted love?"

Roger, who had heard from Phil a description of the Bourke house, now intervened.

"We can be skeptical about the supposed stalking of Madeline Rune and still have a connection between them. He might have wooed her only as a means to an end."

"What end?"

"All those F. X. Bourke materials in the study."

Phil described the study for Waring, who hadn't liked at all the information that there had been a graduate student living in the apartment over the garage at the house where Madeline Rune had been killed and of whose existence he had been unaware. And that Henry Hadley had been with her there until nearly three in the morning. But whatever professional pique he felt dissipated as he and Phil developed the suggestion Roger had made. Over the course of the next fifteen minutes, Henry Hadley came to occupy pride of place among the suspects.

"Of course that isn't all of them," Roger observed.

"Who else? Katherine George, jealous that Madeline was stealing her boyfriend from her?"

"I hadn't thought of that. No, I meant

those cousins of Madeline Rune, the ones with whom she had quarreled over the disposition of the F. X. Bourke papers."

"The Walkers!"

It was Philip who had in his conversation with Madeline learned of the cousins who objected to the sale of the Bourke house, even though they had no legal claim on it. But Katherine George said she had rented the apartment from the Walkers, so they must have been acting for her until she moved back from Chicago. That the accumulated memorabilia of F. X. Bourke should be turned over to the University of Notre Dame was gall and wormwood to them. They had urged the founding of a private museum that would bring thousands upon thousands of paying visitors on home game weekends and attract goodly numbers throughout the years. That such an institution would provide both employment and a residence for the Walkers explained a good part of their interest—and doubtless some measure of Madeline's disinclination to agree. After all, she rented the apartment over the garage precisely in order to keep the Walkers at arm's length. Reminded of this by Roger, Phil nodded slowly.

"You're right, Roger. We can't exclude the Walkers."

As for Waring, he picked up the phone, called one of the detectives assigned to him for this investigation, and gave specific instructions. The first query, of course, concerned where Carey Walker and her husband had been on Saturday night. Or rather, early Sunday morning.

"So there we have it," Philip said with satisfaction. "Either Stanley Rune, Marcus Bramble, Henry Hadley, or the Walkers."

"The Four Losers," Waring said.

"Have we eliminated Phil?" Roger asked, and poured another glass of Chianti while the others laughed. "And don't forget my student, Katherine George."

"I think Hadley is our man," Waring said.

18

Madeline Rune was buried from Sacred
Heart Basilica on campus and the church
was decently full. Half a dozen priests concelebrated with the president; trustees and
members of the various advisory boards
had flown in. Vice-presidents, the provost,
and the deans of the colleges, along with a
sampling of their platoons of associate
deans, assistant deans, and assistants to
the dean—the bureaucratic proliferation in
academe now rivaled that in the public sec-
tor—were in dutiful attendance, but for all
that it was not an affair of the university
community. Few members of the faculty

could even name a trustee, and such lu-
minaries were even more remote from the
student body. Some emeriti were there, if
only to pass the time, and of course the Old
Bastards were represented. Stanley Rune
self-consciously occupied the front pew on
the right.

"The mourners' bench," Ward said in a
stage whisper to Brady.

"No kids?"

Ward shrugged. He had tipped back his
head to study the Gregori paintings high
above them. Brady's eyes had focused on
the painting above what was called the
Lady Chapel, far off behind the main altar.
A beautiful statue of Our Lady, Notre
Dame, stood in an illumined niche, as if to
give her a good view of the whole church.
In the panel painting above she was de-
picted with angels hovering over her, one
suspending a great wreath of flowers above
her head, as if about to crown her. The proportions were all off. If the angel should
drop the wreath, it would slide down over
the Blessed Virgin's shoulders, it was so
large.

"They think he did it." "He" was Stanley
Rune.

Ward's eyes went to the balding man in the front pew. "Each man kills the thing he loves."

"Then he's innocent."

The local paper had all but avoided the story until the coroner's report was made public. Then it grew unctuous about the tragic incident that had robbed both Notre Dame and South Bend of a gracious, civic-minded lady, whose . . . blah blah. . . . The stories might have been written by Lincoln Logan himself. Brady had once been told that obituaries were prepared in advance, and ever since had wondered if an account of his own life was ready to print.

"Know anyone at the *Tribune?*"

"What?"

"Have you got your hearing aid with you?"

"Yes."

"Then put it in."

"It is in."

"Then turn it on."

"What?"

Waring was in the choir loft, keeping an eye on Stanley Rune. Despite what everyone knew, Rune had decided to play the part of the bereaved husband. At the funeral home the night before, Waring had become acquainted with Rune's patter, eavesdropping on his exchange with the president.

"We think we're immortal, don't we, Father?"

"In a sense we are, Stanley."

"How swiftly the years go."

The priest nodded expressionlessly. This was the kind of banality one had to put up with at wakes. Stanley waxed philosophical about the little quarrels that divide husband and wife. "If only we knew."

This was the man whose marriage with Madeline had, by all account, been stormy and unhappy, who had left her and set up separately, who had been catting around after a girl half his age ... and who had very likely killed the woman he professed now to be grieving.

In the pew behind him were the Walkers, she substantial, he diminutive. There was little doubt where the center of gravity in that couple lay. As it happened, it was Waring himself who had spoken with the couple, when he met their plane from Florida upon landing.

"We have a condo in Naples," Mr. Walker said and then was silenced by a look from the center of gravity.

"Why are you meeting our plane?"

"We are looking for any help we can get in the matter of your cousin's murder."

"Murder? The story we heard made it sound like an intruder."

"How did you get the story?"

She gave that a minute's thought. "I talked with Stanley."

"He called you?"

Another pause. "Aren't these odd questions? Perhaps I should simply say that we have been in Florida for the past two weeks, we have not seen my cousin Madeline since August, and I can't imagine any help we could be to you in your investigation."

The other passengers had gone on to the baggage carousels and the Walkers were clearly anxious to get going.

"I'll give you a ride to where you're staying."

She decided that this offer could be accepted without compromise. They had rooms in the Morris Inn. Waring's car was in a No Parking zone just outside the door and so once their bags arrived they were soon on their way.

"You say Stanley Rune told you Madeline had been killed by an intruder?"

"He didn't say that. But he made it sound like an accident."

"I suppose he was pretty broke up."

"They were broken up, Detective Waring. They were separated."

"Even so."

"It had been something of a marriage of convenience."

Mr. Walker snickered and then fell silent. "How so?" Waring asked, and then added, "I should tell you that suspicion has fallen on Stanley."

"I'm not surprised."

With feigned reluctance, Carey Walker spoke of the Rune marriage. There were no children, but of course one mustn't judge on that basis. Sometimes children simply do not come. Mr. Walker stirred, as if to disclaim any responsibility for their lack of offspring.

"You think he might have done it?"

"I'll leave that matter to you professionals."

It was impossible not to see in her manner the renewal of hopes that had been dashed by Madeline Rune. Who were Madeline Rune's heirs?

"Notre Dame," Mario Miranda said, when Waring asked him later that day.

"Entirely?"

"That was her wish and desire. There aren't any relatives. Even if she had still been married to Stanley, they had agreed not to share property."

"Aren't there cousins?"

"The Walkers? Carey Walker was married to a third cousin now deceased. She has married again. She has no claim on the Bourke estate."

It would have been difficult to discern this from Carey Walker's manner. Perhaps there were legal views that differed from Miranda's.

Stanley Rune had smiled when told that he had a reservation at a South Bend motel for Saturday night.

"Of course I have a reservation at the Evergreen. I have one there for every home game of the season and have had for years. Sometimes I use it, sometimes I don't."

Waring had pursued the matter nonetheless and as a result learned that Stanley had been in South Bend on Saturday night. He had attended a post-game party until at least eleven o'clock. But he had returned to his motel at four in the morning.

"You sure about that?" Waring asked the night clerk, who had a habit of moistening his lips and turning his head a degree or two before speaking.

"I am reading *O Pioneers!*"

Waring looked at him.

"It is riveting. Not only was I wide awake reading, I was annoyed at the disturbance. He said he had lost his key."

"Had he picked one up?"

Waring was shown the card Rune had signed when he registered on Saturday morning at ten o'clock. The signature looked like other samples Waring had seen.

Rune was driving a rented car which he had not yet turned in. A check of the odometer indicated that he had put nearly 250 miles on the car, and preliminary conversations with him as to how he had spent the weekend gave no clue as to how or when he could have driven that far. It seemed appropriate to put off questioning Rune until after his wife had been buried— particularly because his whereabouts were never in question. It occurred to Waring that, since he was in church, he might drive all these thoughts from his mind and say a prayer or two.

The Mass completed, the pallbearers began to push the covered coffin slowly down the main aisle. Stanley fell in behind, his face twisted into a tragic mask, as he followed his wife's body from the church. Next came the Walkers. She actually wore a veil and he walked beside her, stiffly self-conscious, his eyes fixed on the floor of the aisle. The pews emptied behind the family and everyone began to file out of the church.

"Is that it?" Philip asked Roger. They were seated in a back pew.

"I think we should go to the cemetery."

"Highland," Father Carmody said. He was wearing street clothes and had every intention of going with the Knight brothers

to the burial. This might have seemed lugubrious if he had not explained. "We can
visit Rockne's grave."

Meanwhile at the scene of the death if
not murder of Madeline Rune, a crew of
three was still at work. Photographs and
fingerprints and the usual tasks of the medical examiner had long since been completed, but this crew had a very definite
objective. A hotel key. Edna Pulchrasky
was in charge, assisted by two uniformed
officers. The area below the veranda was
covered with fallen leaves and the bank of
the river was close enough that it could not
be ruled out that an object dropped or
thrown from the veranda which projected
out toward the river might have ended in
the water. Officer Loring stopped to watch
a chevron of geese go over. Suddenly his
Geiger counter began to click, bringing his
thoughts back to earth. Pulchrasky and Hogan had heard it too and they converged
on the spot. Loring waved them back and
moved his detector with dramatic slowness,
circling carefully until once more the click-
ing began. Hogan was on his knees, carefully removing leaves. A key came

sparkling into view. The three exchanged a silent high-five. It was not often that routine paid off like this.

The key was indeed the key to the room Stanley Rune had rented in the Evergreen Inn east of campus.

19

Miranda, the university counsel, had heard of Roger Knight's desire to visit the Bourke mansion, specifically the collection of sports memorabilia that F. X. had accumulated over the years. Perhaps because he thought of Roger as an envoy of the university, he had urged Polanski to grant the request. Greg Whelan agreed to drive the van which had been designed to make travel easy for Roger.

"Have you ever been to the house, Greg?"

"It's a private home."

Under the circumstances it seemed to

have lost that status. There were several
officers assigned to guard the murder site
and there was yellow tape strung across
the entrance to the porch.

"Drive around back," Roger urged.

He had wanted to see the garages and
the apartment above them ever since first
hearing them described by Philip. When he
had gotten out of the van, an operation that
consumed several minutes, he lumbered
along the side of the garage to the door Phil
had spoken of. There was no indication that
it was the entrance to the stairway leading
to the apartment above, no nameplate, no
doorbell, no mail slot. He opened the door
and looked up the steep stairs with a sinking spirit.

"Want me to go up and see if she's
there?"

He had told Greg of this added reason
for visiting the Bourke house on the drive
out.

"Just tell her Professor Knight is here."

"If she's there."

She was. She came clattering down the
stairs, talking a mile a minute, and ran into
Roger's arms and began babbling that his
brother had been here and now here he

was and wouldn't he come upstairs, she had just made fresh coffee. Roger looked ruefully at the stairway.

"I'd better not."

She was abject; she pleaded with Greg Whelan to persuade Roger. "We'll both help," she promised.

They compromised. She went back upstairs and brought down a thermos of coffee and cups and the three of them went to the main house, where Roger navigated the wide staircase to the second floor without incident. Soon they were in F. X. Bourke's study and a feeling of awe came over them at the sight of all the reminders of past athletic glory and the glorious chronicling of it on the mechanical typewriter that seemed enshrined on the table behind the desk.

Katherine poured coffee and Roger got settled on a vast green leather couch. He was still looking about the room with the glistening eyes of an awestruck youngster. There were those who found the style of F. X. Bourke florid, veering on the baroque, but Roger was not among them. He was prepared to admit that it was no longer the style of sportswriters.

"But, then, sportwriters nowadays are illiterate. Their heads are full of statistics that any fool can call up from a good database."

Greg was perusing the shelves on the wall opposite the desk. He had been told of the novels of William X. McNaughton and soon found them. He brought one to the massive man on the green leather couch— *The Substitute Quarterback*. The dust jacket promised that in these pages the reader would find the saga of Clark Catania, protégé of Lance Lott, who walked onto the practice field during fall practice on the very day that Reynolds, the All American quarterback for the past three years, broke his arm. His backup, Walsh, had the flu. The coach was ready to call it a day when Lance brought Clark forward and introduced him as a quarterback.

"He doesn't know the plays."
"He knows the plays, Coach."
Coach White frowned. "Who gave him a playbook?"
But Clark had diagrammed the plays for the past two years as a spectator. He knew everything but their call signals.

Lance said he would give Clark the number of the play he wanted to call.

"Give it a try."

Clark's debut had been memorable and his future looked bright.

"Yours is a God-given talent, son," Coach White said solemnly.

But Walsh recovered and was given the quarterback spot. Reynolds' injury proved to be less serious than originally diagnosed. Through a long season, Clark watched Walsh lead the team from one close victory to another. In the final home game, Walsh was knocked unconscious with the team behind by ten points. Clark went in and in five minutes had erased the deficit and then gone on to add twenty-one points. The last game of the season was scheduled in California two weeks later, Reynolds was recovered and the great question was: Would Reynolds or Clark Catania play quarterback in the final game that would decide the season for Lawrenceville?

Roger looked up. "Phil was right. McNaughton is good. I mean from a boy's point of view."

Greg Whelan said, "It is going to be a

tremendous job cataloguing all this into the archives."

"It seems a shame to move anything."

Katherine agreed and an idea formed in Roger's mind, an idea he followed up on as soon as he was back in his campus apartment. Marcus Bramble had given him a number where he could always be reached, and in a minute Roger was talking to the prosperous entrepreneur and owner of several professional athletic franchises in different sports and whose devotion to Knute Rockne seemed to know no bounds.

"I have been thinking of the Rockne Museum," Roger began. He outlined the chain of thoughts that had been triggered by his visit to the Bourke mansion. It was not unusual for the study or office of a great personage to be taken apart and reassembled in a museum, somewhat like the way the Rockefellers had brought The Cloisters to New York. A feature of presidential libraries was a replica of the Oval Office in the White House, where the former chief executive had made his claim on the attention of his fellow citizens. The University of Texas had brought the workroom of Erle Stanley Gardner to the Austin campus and made it a centerpiece of its Gardner collection.

"You want a sportswriter's study to be the centerpiece of a Rockne museum?"

"Certainly not. He would be a moon, reflecting the principal light of the great coach. I think we should pursue your original idea and have Rockne's grave transferred to campus. Do you know Les Invalides?"

"Tell me about him."

Roger smoothly conveyed that it was a place not a person, the site of Napoleon's grave, which drew thousands upon thousands of tourists every year.

"I had been thinking of the church."

"Churches are for saints, Marcus. Rockne was a good man, no doubt, but his influence is in the world of sports. I imagine the grave in a large circular room. An oval railing will permit visitors to look down at the simple stone beneath which Rockne lies at rest."

Roger's mind was full of Les Invalides, of course, but his enthusiasm proved contagious and soon Bramble was caught up in the idea. "Whereabouts on campus, Professor?"

"You know St. Joseph's Lake?"

"The one to the east?"

"Yes. There is a small island."

Roger waited as the image formed in the mind of Marcus Bramble. A tasteful edifice, neoclassical in design, the work of Thomas Gordon Smith, the head of the Architecture School, would be built on that island. Access would be easy. Visitors might stop at the grotto before or after viewing the Rockne exhibit.

They talked for half an hour, Bramble refusing to take other phone calls that demanded his attention. And at the end he said he was flying to South Bend so they could nail this down.

"The team plays in Ann Arbor this weekend," Roger warned, in case Bramble thought it was a home date.

"We can fly up for it. No problem. But we will have more opportunities for extended discussion without the distraction of a game on campus."

"Let us hope no one gets killed this weekend," Roger said cheerfully.

20

Phil went to Chicago with Waring when the detective confronted Stanley Rune with the motel key that had been found at the scene of the murder. Stanley dismissed it as a mere bagatelle.

"Madeline knew of that standing reservation. She made it available to friends as often as I did."

"You're suggesting that a guest of hers used the motel room last Saturday?"

"That key could have been where you found it for weeks."

"The clerk remembers your coming in at

four in the morning and asking for a key because you had lost yours."

Stanley laughed. "That clerk must have a very good memory."

"Do you deny it?"

"Of course I deny it. Look, detective, if you think finding a motel key at Bourke house is a basis for suspecting me of doing harm to my wife, I suggest you proceed."

Waring had not been prepared for such a carefree reaction, and Phil could see the policeman considering the relative weight of testimony from the confident Stanley Rune and that from the motel clerk who had seemed as eager to talk of Willa Cather as of guests rolling in at four in the morning. That clerk had not been on duty the following day and no one had formally checked out of the motel.

"How do you pay for that reservation?"

"They bill me."

"Even when you don't use the room?"

"Why should they care?" Of course it went without saying that paying for a room he did not use meant little to the affluent Rune.

"You did go to the game, didn't you?"

"Yes."

"What did you do afterward?"

"Returned to Chicago."

"What time was that?"

"After the game."

"Immediately."

"I had something to eat before leaving. It's always best to wait for the traffic to thin out before getting on the road."

"Where did you eat?"

"With a friend."

"Where."

"At my friend's house."

Stanley Rune's manner perceptibly changed when Waring began questioning him about what he had done after the game. Waring asked for the friend's name. Rune shook his head.

"What is the point of these questions?"

"You know the point."

"Are you accusing me of killing my wife?"

"It is as much a matter of seeing if we can exclude you as a possible suspect. I would appreciate your providing me with anything and everything that might do that."

"When was Madeline killed?"

"Between three and four in the morning."

"And at four o'clock someone claiming to be me showed up at the Evergreen Inn and said he had lost the key to the room."

"That's right."

"At four o'clock I was here in Chicago, in my apartment, asleep."

"In that case, you have nothing to worry about."

"I'm not worried in the least."

"Is there some way I could verify that?"

"I don't see how. I sleep alone."

It was that addendum that caught Phil's attention and, as he learned after they had left Rune's office, Waring's as well. Madeline had described Stanley as a womanizer, so this prim protestation of chastity rang false.

"I think you were wise not to pursue the matter now. You will need a bushel basket full of evidence to shake that man's aplomb."

This was an implicit criticism, but Phil left it implicit. He had not imagined that Waring had gone all the way to Chicago with only the key found at the Bourke house as a lever to pry a confession out of Stanley Rune. Rune, after all, was a lawyer, and accusations and situations that might unhinge the layman were factors of his daily life. Police inquiries were very far from a charge and a charge from a grand jury indictment, and many things might intervene before anything like a trial began. A layman might see himself in the dock immediately with a hostile court eager to convict him. Rune had not even imagined that he would want to consult with another legal mind about the questions Waring put to him.

"Well, that was a waste of time."

"Why don't we have some lunch and then check out Rune's apartment."

"We should have done that first."

They had a very large meal at Berghof's, and Phil would have liked a nap afterward, but stepping into the brisk wind as they left the restaurant brought back the desire to find out what they could about Stanley Rune's domestic circumstances in Chicago.

North of the river near Waterfront but several blocks west of the lake shore is an area of the city that draws young people, both as residents and as patrons of the stores and restaurants: single women sharing an apartment and walking back and forth to the Loop in gym shoes, young bankers on the bottom rung and equally young lawyers new to one large firm or another. After dark, when the Loop is forbidding and abandoned, this area is bright and alive with activity. Music of unusual sorts emanates from club and café, the songs of youthful revelry are not unheard, a general air of bohemian unrestraint is dominant. It was in this chic countercultural area fashioned for those in the most staid occupations that Stanley Rune lived. On side streets were to be found multiple-resident dwellings dating from the twenties, flats with large rooms and high ceilings and great windows looking onto the street.

Finding a parking space on the curb in front of Stanley Rune's address was impossible, and after several circlings of the block in the wan hope of finding an empty spot, Phil proposed that he hop out and make inquiries while Waring continued to look for a place to park. Their difficulty had suggested an opening. Horns began to complain during the short time it took Phil to get out and he slapped the car as a signal for Waring to move on.

He managed to squeeze between parked cars to the sidewalk where he stood and admired the house in which Stanley Rune dwelt. Had Madeline shared this place with him or had he moved here after the breakup? Charming as the building was, the neighborhood seemed inappropriate for her. But for an aging Lothario, the sight and sound of all that youth might prove aphrodisiac. A stairway led up to the wide entry door, which was flanked by windows and had a fanlight above it. On either side, pairs of high, wide windows observed the street. There were two full stories and a third floor as well. A wrought-iron fence protected the brief lawn, and Phil went through the gate and then followed the walk that went around to the side of the house. There was not much space between this building and the next and he had the feeling that he was going through a tunnel, but at the back he found what he was looking for—stairs leading to a basement door on which MANAGER was written. He went on down and knocked.

"Just a minute," someone called from within and in a moment the door opened and a woman backed out, then turned, keeping the door open with her hip, while she proceeded to transfer the armful of clothing to Phil. When he backed away, she looked at him in puzzlement.

"What's wrong?"

"I didn't come for those?"

"You're not Zephyr Cleaners?" Puzzlement gave way to annoyance.

"I wanted to talk with you about this building."

She was not what he would have expected to find behind a door named Manager. She was in her twenties, with thick auburn hair pulled back on her head and secured with a green band. She wore a rust-colored baggy sweater and slacks. And she was losing her grip on the clothes she had tried to give him and then had to take back. First one garment, then another got away, and when she clutched what was left more tightly, she moved and the door began to close. Phil lunged to stop it from closing, managing to knock the rest of the clothes from her arms. Behind her the door clicked shut. At her feet lay the garments meant for Zephyr Cleaners. Her eyes sparked with annoyance as she looked at Phil, then she turned and tried to open the now-locked door.

"I'm sorry," he said.

Her mouth was a line made by in-drawn lips, her brow knitted, and she looked at him and then suddenly began to laugh.

"It's not your fault. You don't even look like Zephyr Cleaners."

Together they picked up the clothes and then faced one another, each holding half the burden.

"Can you get in?"

She grew serious. "What is it you wanted?"

"This is going to sound silly."

"I hope so."

He said, honestly enough, that passing by the house had brought on a sudden desire to find out about it, to see if there was any possibility . . .

"Of buying one of the apartments?" She shook her head. "There is a list and there hasn't been a sale for ages."

"Have you been here for ages?"

"Just a year. I'm a student. I'm filling in for my uncle, who's in the hospital."

She kept looking at the closed door and Phil wondered how she would get back inside.

"Where do people park?"

"At the end of the block around the corner on State."

"Actually I know someone who lives here."

"Who?"

"Stanley Rune."

Something happened to her expression. In a bold move Phil got out his wallet and showed her his license. "What I said about the house is true, but that isn't the reason I'm here."

"You're a detective."

"That's right. I don't know if you've heard that Stanley Rune's wife—his estranged wife—was killed in South Bend last Saturday night."

Her mouth opened in surprise. "Killed?"

"Rune was down there for the football game but says he returned to Chicago afterward."

She was nodding. "He did. He got back on Sunday morning."

"What time was that?"

"Nine, ten o'clock. Look, I'm freezing. Turn the other way."

He did and heard the doormat move. Obviously a key was kept beneath the mat. In a moment the door opened and he followed her inside.

It was the kitchen. He put the clothes he carried on the table and asked her if she was sure that Stanley Rune had returned from South Bend in the midmorning on Sunday.

"The papers are all delivered here and I take them around to the apartments. No need to do that very early. They all sleep late on Sunday. I had just left Mr. Rune's at his door when he came upstairs, unshaven, smelling of booze. He wanted to tell me all about the game he had seen in South Bend."

"You realize this is very important."

"Do you think that he killed his wife?"

"It's not impossible. Your testimony could be crucial."

"Oh, my God." And then she said, "Ask at the garage. They'll know when he got back."

"Give me the address."

The thought that the burden of Stanley Rune's guilt or innocence would repose on her testimony made her eager to comply. Phil took the slip and then there was a knock on the door and this time it was

Zephyr Cleaners. He helped her put the clothes in the laundry bag the man carried.

"You've been a tremendous help."

"Not to Mr. Rune."

"If he's innocent, you can't hurt him."

"He's not the innocent type."

Waring had circled the block a dozen times and had begun to think that Phil had deserted him.

"I thought you stood me up."

"And have to take the South Shore back? Around the corner we'll find the garage where Rune keeps his car."

"He rented a car in South Bend."

"When was it turned in?"

"He had them pick it up at the Evergreen."

"So he must have driven his own car back here."

There was a little raised walkway on one side of the descending circular ramp and at the bottom was a glass-enclosed office where the attendant sat. Philip showed the man his license and was answered with a lidded, skeptical look.

"We want to ask you about one of your clients."

"Why should I tell you anything?"

Twenty dollars proved insufficient reason and twenty more did not help. When the man still shook his head when four twenties lay on the desk between them, Phil reached to scoop them up, but the attendant's hand got there first. "How can I help you?"

"What kind of records do you keep of the coming and going of cars."

"Long-term renters?"

"Yes."

"What do you want to know?"

"When Stanley Rune put his car away here last Sunday morning."

"Morning! It was nearly noon."

"How do you know that?"

"I was here."

"What makes you remember?"

"Because the SOB almost never tips. He left his car right there, just waved and walked up the ramp."

"You've been a great help." Phil put another twenty on the desk. "We'll be in touch."

"What's he done?"

"Failed to tip."

21

Confronted with the discrepancies in his story, Stanley Rune, having listened carefully, reached for his telephone and put through a call to South Bend, engaging Manfred Dosch to represent him. He nodded in response to questions inaudible to Waring and Phil Knight and then put down the phone.

"On advice of counsel, I will say nothing now in response to these absurd charges. Am I under arrest?"

"You are neither charged nor under arrest. Yet. I felt it fair to tell you of the things we have learned that suggest that you have been less than candid with me."

"I can't discuss them with you."

"I will add, then, that you are our chief suspect and that we will not be keeping that a secret."

Rune had joined his hands while Waring spoke. Now he separated them, palms upward, as if inviting them to join him in prayer.

"You told us that you returned to Chicago only hours after the game. We have two witnesses who place your return to Chicago at midmorning Sunday. You said you did not make use of the room you had rented in the Evergreen Inn, yet the clerk remembers your entry at four o'clock when you asked for a key to the room, having lost your own. A key to the room in the Evergreen Inn was found at the scene of the killing. I will not go into the unhappy relationship you had with your former wife."

"Circumstantial," Rune observed.

Waring did not contest this. On the way down in the elevator, he expressed doubt whether he should have warned Stanley Rune that suspicion was now focused on him.

"It was absolutely the right thing to do,"

Phil said. He had urged this course on Waring when they emerged from the garage. "I
will remain here and see what if anything
our suspect does in response to your visit."

They parted in the lobby of the building
in which Stanley Rune had his law office.
Phil watched Waring push through the re-
volving doors into the windy out-of-doors.
Phil then crossed the lobby to a café where,
sipping coffee at a counter stool, he was
able to keep an eye on the elevators. Of
course there would be several ways in
which Rune could exit the building unob-
served, and in other circumstances Phil
would have informed himself of all the possibilities and taken appropriate precautions.
But the very manner in which Waring had
passed on his suspicions to Rune had been
disarming. Worried the man might be, but
he was unlikely to think that he was under
surveillance. After all, it was his past deeds
that were being scrutinized.

His cup had been refilled a second time
when he saw Stanley Rune come out of the
elevator and head in a straight line for the
street door. His topcoat was unbuttoned
and fluttered about him, his chin was thrust

forward, and he wore a concentrated look. Phil spun off the stool and went in pursuit of his quarry.

Rune had gone north a few doors and was now on the curb, looking for a cab. His expression was one of impatience. With a shake of his head, he lowered his arm and began to walk north with swinging arms and long stride. Phil followed and the wind was fresh in his face, bringing tears to his eyes, but he welcomed this decision of Rune's. His daily exercising in the Loftus Center was insufficient and the apartment could not easily accommodate the NordicTrak that he had left behind in Rye. Unless he was mistaken, Rune intended to walk the several miles to his apartment and Phil relished the thought. It almost made him want to catch up with Rune so that they could enjoy the walk together.

It was odd being more a spectator than a participant in an investigation, he thought. Waring did a fairly good job with what he had, and he himself had suggested laying out for Rune where he now stood in the investigation. He hadn't added that he would then see what this information would precipitate. If he had any objection to Waring's procedure it was its passivity. A private investigator is more likely to try to make new things happen that will cast light on what originally spurred the investigation. Despite the circumstantial case against Rune, Phil had his doubts, doubts that had been generated by a conversation the night before with Roger.

His obese brother had been full of his visit to the study of F. X. Bourke and spoke of it to Phil as if he had not been there first. But, then, Roger's photographic recall of the room made Phil wonder if he had actually seen it when he himself was there.

"Rockne is the key, Phil," Roger had said, turning forty-five degrees in the chair he had brought from Rye. It was a chair he spent the day in, one he had designed himself and had built at considerable expense. In it, he became mobile, moving with grace around the great room in which he worked. That room was recalled here by that chair, despite the reduced dimensions of the room in which they sat.

"The key to what?"

"The murder of Madeline Rune."

"How so?"

Roger put an index finger to his chin and

his gaze became unfocused. "I'm not sure."

That the ghost of Rockne had been present from the beginning of the sequence in which Madeline Rune had met her death was clear, but there seemed no way a causal connection could be established between Marcus Bramble's decision to commemorate Rockne in what he deemed a fitting way and Madeline's death. True, it had happened in her family home, the Bourke house, and equally true, F. X. Bourke had been a teammate of Rockne as an undergraduate and later as a sportswriter was the man most responsible for bringing Rockne to the attention of the nation. But such links were of the kind that Roger on any other occasion would call *per accidens*. What possible connection could there be between a wealthy alumnus's announcement that he wanted to build a memorial to Knute Rockne on the campus of Notre Dame and the killing of the granddaughter of his former teammate and later Boswell?

Rune had now reached the Chicago River and was striding even more vigorously as he went across the bridge with Phil following. Phil calculated that they were halfway there, then drove the thought from his mind. That made it appear that he could not wait for this invigorating walk to be over. The cold air in his lungs, the wind stinging his eyes, the numbness in his legs told him he was out of shape, but there was Rune, at least ten years older, moving along like a gazelle. Phil called on his hidden resources and stepped up the pace. Rune's reaction to the news that he was the prime suspect in the death of his former wife seemed to be to insure his own longevity by this punishing walk into the Chicago wind.

When they turned into the street where Rune lived, Phil fell back. Rune was on the opposite side of the street, the side on which his building stood, and Phil let the diagonal distance between them increase. Rune skipped up the steps to the large front door and let himself in. Phil continued along the opposite side of the street to a point where he could see the window of Rune's apartment. The light did not go on, but soon Stanley was visible, moving about inside. The light went on in a room farther back from the street, and from time to time Phil was aware of Rune's flitting shadow. Then the light went off. Phil pressed his back against the building and waited.

Minutes went by, five, then ten. Phil had assumed that Rune would be coming out again, but the large front door did not open. Fifteen minutes later, he crossed the street and went around to the back, where he knocked on the door of the manager's apartment.

"You again!" But she said it with a smile.

"I forgot to ask your name."

"Why do you have to know my name?"

"For my report." She said her name was Janet Blair.

"I am worried about Stanley Rune."

"You are?"

"He's in his apartment and I'm afraid something might have happened to him . . ."

"He's not in his apartment."

"Are you sure?"

"He left not ten minutes ago."

Phil made a face. "Then I just missed him. Look, can I ask you an incredible favor."

The favor was to let him into Stanley Rune's apartment. Perhaps if they had not gone through the business with the dry cleaner and her armful of clothes, she would have simply said no. Perhaps if she were her uncle, who had experience in such matters, she would have simply said no. She didn't say no, simply or otherwise. She asked why he wanted to see Mr. Rune's apartment when he wasn't home.

"I'd rather not say, Janet. You understand. Look, come with me. It will only take a few minutes."

"He really isn't there."

"In a way it's better that he isn't."

"You know, you don't make a whole lot of sense."

"It's the nature of my work."

That made so little sense that she accepted it. She took a ring of keys with her and they went up an inner stairway and soon were at the door of Stanley Rune's apartment.

"My uncle would kill me if he knew I was doing this."

"Don't mention killing, please."

Her mouth rounded. "His wife," she whispered.

She unlocked the door and they went in. He wasn't two steps inside the door when he saw what he had not known he had come for, but he did not let on. He stepped aside, to let her lead the way, but she shook her head. "I've never been here before. Can you hurry?"

He walked through the rooms, certain that they had been furnished and decorated by Madeline. The only masculine room was a den with a television set whose screen seemed as large as a wall of the room. Stanley smoked at home obviously; the room had the acrid odor of departed cigars. There was another photograph here, matching that he had seen when he first came in.

"Find what you're looking for?"

He shook his head. "But that's what I expected."

She dropped her chin to her chest. "You're crazy."

"Where should we go for dinner?"

"I'm on duty! I can't go anywhere." But she half smiled and looked speculatively at him. Perhaps she had never thought of herself before as attracted to older men.

"We'll have something brought in."

Pasquale's, around the corner, brought in spaghetti carbonara, saltimbocca romana, a salad, and a bottle of Barolo. They ate at the kitchen table, where he listened to the story of her efforts to finish her degree.

"I dread turning thirty without completing it."

"That gives you lots of time."

She gave him a look from the corner of her eye. She could be in her mid twenties. Her college career had been desultory because she had had to drop out several times in order to earn enough money to return to Loyola.

"What's your major?"

"Criminology."

"Come on."

"I'm serious. It's a branch of sociology."

He imagined what Roger would say to someone expending years in the study of so ephemeral a subject as criminology.

"Do you know what Father Brown said to Sherlock Holmes?"

"Who's Father Brown?"

Roger would have given her a little lecture on the difference between a bogus rationalism and judgments through connaturality, but Phil wasn't sure he could bring it off. Besides, she didn't know Roger and he was happy to enjoy her unfeigned interest in himself. As a budding criminologist, she wanted to know of the life of a private investigator. It was pleasant to give her his own version of his professional exploits. Inevitably he mentioned Roger and inevitably she said she would love to meet his enormous brother.

"He can't be as large as you claim."

That she would have to verify for herself. Two hours went by, Rune had not returned, and he received from Janet the assurance that she would keep an eye on the tenant and keep Phil posted. He gave her a card, writing on it his South Bend number.

"Rye, New York," she read in wondering tones, looking at the printed legend. "Is there really such a place?"

22

"I read them all," Father Quirk said when Roger asked him about the novels of William X. McNaughton.

"The Substitute Quarterback?"

"Clark Catania," the ancient priest said after a moment's thought. "One of his best."

"I had never heard of them."

"You know the stories of Father Finn?"

"I believe you mentioned them before."

"Wonderful books. Just the kind of thing boys ought to read. Not as good as McNaughton, of course. Sports were not a big thing with Finn. McNaughton understood a boy's mind better."

"How would you rank Rockne compared with those two?"

"The Four Winners?" Quirk's eyes were large and bright in his hairless face. "You say you've read it?"

"Yes."

"What did you think?"

"What did Doctor Johnson say of the dog who played the violin?"

"I don't know."

"It was not that he played it well but that he played it at all that amazed one."

Quirk emitted a cackling laugh and nodded his skull-like head. "That's good. And that's about it, isn't it? The only good parts are when a game is in progress."

"He could have learned a lot from his former teammate. About writing."

"Bourke tried to help. Look, it might have been worse."

"Was that the only one he wrote?"

"It was the only one that got published. Anything with Rock's name on it was surefire, of course. What's Bramble up to?"

"Now he's thinking of funding a Rockne

museum, a place where all the memorabilia could be brought together. F. X. Bourke left his papers to the university."

When Roger told the old priest of the plan to build the museum on St. Joseph's Lake, he added, "You'll be able to see it from your window."

"They'll have to hurry up and build it for that to happen."

"F. X. Bourke's study will be rebuilt in the museum. And Rockne's grave will be there, too."

"He check with the family?"

"Mario Miranda, the university lawyer, is looking into that."

"I can't believe that the administration is cooperating with this."

The change in attitude had come with the publicity surrounding the murder of a Notre Dame trustee. News about Rockne was sure to eclipse any other Notre Dame news, so the administration had begun to treat Marcus Bramble differently.

"They might fight the idea of the island location, though."

"What alternative do they suggest?"

"They have appointed a committee."

*   *   *

Roger wasn't sure how much Father Quirk knew about the death of Madeline Rune and Father Carmody could not enlighten him on this. But, then, Father Carmody's grasp on what was going on about him was uncertain: the present simply did not adhere to his memory as the past had done.

"Her father died in Korea," Father Carmody said, speaking of Madeline Rune.

F. X. Bourke had married late, after Rockne's death. His wife had served as his secretary for several years, the first female assistant he had had, and he was surprised by how companionable she was. They married and had a son and F. X. had been heard to lament that his wife would be left to raise their child, actuarial tables being what they were. But she died in her early forties and he was still alive when word came that his son had been killed near Pusan. His daughter-in-law, Madeline's mother, moved into the Bourke house, and it was there that Madeline had been raised. Her memories of her grandfather could not have been vivid; she was not yet five when he died. On the other hand, her life had been lived in a house that had increasingly become a shrine to her grandfather. Madeline's mother, who had filled the same role her husband's mother had before her, saw how valuable the keepsakes and mementos and papers of a long lifetime were, and she had insured that F. X.'s study was preserved exactly as he had left it.

"Why not just move the whole house over to the island?" Father Quirk's smile was like half a piano keyboard.

The head archivist, while she was professionally covetous and longed to take possession of the F. X. Bourke papers, did not like this talk of housing them somewhere other than the archives.

"What Mr. Bramble should be doing is thinking archives," she complained. "If we had a proper building, we could highlight the Rockne papers and anything else he wants and have plenty of room for everything else as well."

The administration did not encourage her suggestion. Media coverage of Marcus Bramble's generosity to his alma mater had driven out of the public eye all news of the ongoing investigation into the violent death of one of Notre Dame's trustees. As between murder of its officers and attention to the university's extraordinary athletic record and its enormous debt to Knute Rockne, there was no contest. Marcus Bramble flew in for a photo op with the president and fielded questions afterward.

"Where are you going to bury Rockne, Father?"

"The intention is to praise him," the president said, then smiled enigmatically. He had the sense of quoting something, but he wasn't sure what it was. He had majored in accounting and studied theology in a third world country from which he returned to campus to streamline the university's finances.

"Why not a hall of the coaches, Mr. Bramble? Rockne and Leahy and Ara and all the rest?"

"Gerry?"

Appreciative snickering. But Bramble did not want to strike a cynical note. He grew sober. "If this university has a future, it will lie in following the lead of Knute Rockne. The athletic program should set the tone for Notre Dame in the future as it did in the past."

The president gripped the donor's arm and smiled as if he had arthritis of the jaw. Mercifully, the media thought they had enough. In fact, they wondered why the conference had been called.

"We already covered this," a print reporter groused.

"Have you ever heard of a pet Rockne?"

Bramble asked about the investigation into Madeline's death after the cameras had been shut down and the reporters had drifted away.

"I'll have Mario Miranda brief you, Marcus."

"What's he got to do with it?"

"The police keep him informed."

"I'll check with the police."

Waring told Bramble that they were about to make an arrest.

"Who?"

"Stanley Rune."

"He did it?"

"That's what it looks like."

Bramble listened open-mouthed to the list of circumstantial evidence. The lying about when he returned to Chicago, the lost room key that necessitated asking the desk clerk for another at four in the morning, the discovery of the missing key at the scene of the murder.

"He had threatened to harm her," Bramble said. "She told me that the night it happened."

Waring nodded. Others had heard the same story from Madeline Rune.

"What are you waiting for?"

Waring leaked the story to the *South Bend Tribune*, which had shown little interest in the sequel of Madeline Rune's death. The story was picked up in Chicago and the word was out. The South Bend police were about to make an arrest in the matter of the death of Madeline Rune. Every indication was that it was her estranged husband, Stanley, who would be charged with her death.

This news story had three unlooked-for consequences.

The first was Pamela Menucci calling the paper to say that there was no mystery at all about where Stanley Rune was until four o'clock Sunday morning. He was with her.

Mobile units for local television sped to her home, and the young woman, standing tall and impassive and looking the camera right in the lens, said that she was in love with Stanley Rune and he was in love with her. They had gone to the game together and afterward to a party. Then they had spent hours in a room in a local motel.

"The Evergreen Inn?"

She nodded. "Yes."

But the desk clerk at the Evergreen Inn, when he saw Stanley Rune's picture on television, put in a call to Detective Waring.

"I told you that Stanley Rune came to the desk and asked for a key because he had lost his?"

"At four in the morning."

"That was the time. But it wasn't the man whose picture they showed on television. If that is a picture of Stanley Rune, the man who told me he was Stanley Rune was someone else."

When Pamela Menucci was asked if she was sure it had been Stanley Rune she spent those hours with in the Evergreen Inn, she burst into tears. Her father picked up a rake and drove the reporters from his yard. The enraged countenance of Professor Menucci was featured in all news stories on these unfolding events.

In Chicago, Stanley denied having an affair with Pamela Menucci and then seemed to disappear. Waring and a county prosecutor called on Stanley's address in the company of local law enforcement officers, but the lawyer was not at home. The manager of the building in which he lived said she had not seen him all day.

"Except on television. I saw the nice things he said about that girl."

His car was not in the garage where he usually kept it and a discreet APB went out, asking Illinois and Indiana troopers to keep an eye out for his licence plate. Wisconsin troopers were added as an afterthought. Days went by and neither Stanley nor his car were sighted.

It was Katherine George who discovered his body. He lay in shallow water just below the veranda of the Bourke house, his torso lapped by the lazy waters of the St. Joseph River. He had died of violence. Indeed the wound on the back of his head was remarkably like that on his wife's. "His and Hers," Artaud, an assistant to the medical examiner, murmured.

The cause of death and the nature of the wound were much mentioned during the following hours. The common assumption that Stanley, cornered by the investigators into his wife's death, had taken his own life was of course negated by the way he had actually died. Nonetheless, the unstated thought was that he had died under a cloud.

"No, under water," Artaud corrected.

This was not a quip. Stanley had been struck on the back of the head and had fallen forward into the water. But it was not the blow that had killed him; it was the quantities of river water that filled his lungs and choked off breathing. Stanley Rune had drowned.

23

In the days that followed, Pamela Menucci seemed to have taken her cue from the mysterious woman who had for years visited the grave of Rudolph Valentino on the anniversary of his death. She was silent, she was regal, she was inconsolable. And she was an irresistible target of the media. Her performance suggested that the death of Stanley Rune was linked to the grand passion the two of them had shared. Luigi Menucci came to Roger Knight to beg for his help.

"Sediamoci," Roger suggested. *"Per favore."*

But the restless professor of Italian continued to move rapidly back and forth across the room. Finally Roger, no longer able to bear the burdens of a host, sank into his specially made chair and wheeled out of the path of Menucci's pacing. Nor did he venture further into the language of which Menucci was a master. Menucci spoke a beautiful if formal English that added pathos to his tale.

"She is her mother all over again, Professor. The sins of parents are indeed visited on their children. And now the police wish to visit her imaginary sins on me. I think they believe that I exacted a father's revenge on the man who stole his daughter's honor."

"They have accused you of killing Stanley Rune?"

"Would that they would." And Roger could almost hear Menucci explain that this apparent double subjunctive was nothing of the kind. "A clear statement I could confront. No, it is insinuation, innuendo, inferences not quite drawn that leave me helpless. Where was I at such and such an hour on Thursday night? How well informed

am I about my daughter's private life. Of
course it is all Horst."

"Horst?"

"German," Menucci said disdainfully.
"An alleged colleague of mine. He is always coming to me with tales about my
daughter and one man or another. I tell him
this is America, the land of the free, where
fathers are comic characters and the family
a fading memory. He has no sense of hu-
mor. I believe he himself has designs on
Pamela, ludicrous as you will find the suggestion."

"Did Horst speak to the police?"

"That is why I have come to you! Your
brother, I am told, is a private investigator.
You must beg him to become involved in
this matter. A lawyer can do me no good
because they accuse me of nothing. Not
yet. Is your brother here?"

Roger reached Phil at the Loftus Center
and asked when he could return to speak
with Professor Menucci.

"The girl's father?"

"That's right."

"Give me ten minutes."

Fifteen minutes passed before Phil came

in the door and in the meantime Roger tried
to calm Menucci by turning to other topics,
to the gossip that is the *élan vital* of the
academic life, but Menucci shrugged away
the topic of Marcus Bramble and his plan
for a Rockne museum.

"Isn't your daughter an architect?"

"After this, who knows?"

"Mr. Bramble may set the task of design-
ing the museum to the fifth-year architecture students."

"She is not going to classes. She is pursued by journalists. She is behaving like an
angel!"

He meant her silence, however ambiguous its effects. Her mother had longed to
be an actress. Earlier she had hoped to
sing, to act in opera, but alas her voice. . . .
Menucci's remarks about his late wife con-
jured up a romantic figure in quest of un-
attainable objects who had cast herself for
roles she was not destined to play, thereby
defining her life as a noble failure.

"She lost the will to live. She decided to
die. Not consciously, perhaps, but the world
was too much with her."

His great almond eyes were awash in

tears. He was dabbing at them when Phil came in.

Waring had been working out with Phil at Loftus, so Phil was able to bring both Roger and their visitor up to date on the death of Stanley Rune. Shortly before noon on Friday, Stanley had taken his car from the garage in Chicago where he always parked it. The story that told the world he was a suspect in his wife's death had broken Thursday night. It was mid morning on Friday that Pamela had dropped her bombshell, to be followed by the further and contradictory bombshell of the desk clerk at the Evergreen Inn. The man who had shown up at the Inn at four in the morning the previous Sunday claiming to be Stanley Rune and asking for a key to his room was not Stanley Rune. Rune had been confronted with the original story when he arrived at his office shortly after nine o'clock on Friday morning. After an hour and a half of media harassment, he had escaped. If he had gone to his apartment, he would have been waylaid once again by the media. But he headed for the garage and drove out at 11:50 A.M. The estimated time of death was

mid to late afternoon on Friday. The drive
from Chicago to South Bend takes two
hours, more or less, so Stanley Rune had
been in South Bend only a few hours before someone struck him on the back of the
head, causing him to fall forward into the
shallow water along the bank of the St. Joseph River and drown. Waring's question
was the obvious one. Why would anyone
want to kill Stanley Rune? Thus far, the media had opted for the motive of revenge,
and that put Menucci on the spot.

"Did you tell them where you were on Friday afternoon?"

"They don't believe me."

"What did you tell them?"

"I visited the grotto, I walked around the
lakes, I returned to the grotto." His face became more tragic. "It was the anniversary
of my wedding. We would have been married thirty-nine years."

"Was there anything between your
daughter and Stanley Rune?"

Menucci tapped his forehead with his
surprisingly elegant hand. "In her head
only. She was her mother all over again."

In this, it turned out, Menucci was mistaken. His colleague Horst might be a gos-

sip, but in the case of Pamela Menucci and Stanley Rune he had been telling the truth. Perhaps, to give him credit, he thought he owed it to the father to tell him.

"He knows it's true," Horst told Roger in the cloakroom of the University Club. "Why does he deny it?"

"That he killed Stanley Rune?"

Horst laughed derisively. "That is ridiculous."

If Menucci chose to believe that his daughter's infatuation with Stanley Rune was only in her head, his own rejection of the facts represented a less credible wishful thinking. Still, there was something noble about a father refusing to believe ill of his daughter. But there was a good deal of imagining in the police investigation as well. Roger went into the club dining room, where Greg Whelan awaited him. In return for lunch, Whelan would drive the van with Roger in it back to the library so he could spend the afternoon in the archives.

Whelan's quest for Rockne's contract with Devin-Adair and of royalty reports from publisher to author had so far been fruitless. He had put together a profile of the man to whom the novel was dedicated, Arnold J. McInerny, who had played football with Rockne and F. X. Bourke. The prospect of taking custody of the Bourke papers made Whelan salivate, but recent developments had made him anxious.

"Our claim on the papers may be clouded by the death of both Madeline and Stanley Rune. Or so I am told."

"I thought it was a bequest in F. X. Bourke's will."

"It is. But there is a trust clause as well which delayed delivery and gave custody to his granddaughter until she should choose to turn over the papers."

"And she was about to do that when she died."

"About to," Whelan intoned. "Those fateful words. I could tell you stories."

He had several instances of donors who in the crunch found it all but impossible to turn over to the university what they had given.

"Often they have delusions of the monetary value of the items. Absurd, of course. What do you suppose Rockne items would bring at auction? And we are talking of far less famous individuals. It is worse in the case of books."

"How so?"

"Amateurs tend to think that all old books are valuable and are certain that they are being misled. Not long ago, there was a tax break involved in such gifts and we had to provide an estimate of value. Even the most liberal estimate would be met by wailing. How could a book published in 1903 fail to be worth thousands?"

There are joys and pains in every profession and Roger was more fascinated than bored by Whelan's account of the perils of the archivist. They went on to the library, where Roger spent an enjoyable afternoon rummaging through odds and ends of the Rockne papers. He could appreciate Whelan's expectation that the juxtaposition of the Bourke and Rockne papers would open new vistas.

Henry Hadley came in around three, greeted Roger coldly, and settled down to work. Of course Hadley would include Roger in the hatred he felt for Philip.

24

Examination of the site where Stanley Rune's body was found turned up a surprising fact. The medical examiner was now doubtful in the extreme that the victim had been struck down where the body was found. There were unmistakable signs that the body had been dragged to the water's edge and allowed to fall forward into the water. His conjecture was that the body had been dragged from a point on the circular driveway to the river's edge.

"So it could have been brought there in a car?"

Waring only lifted his brows. "There has

been so much traffic to and from the Bourke house of late it would be very difficult to distinguish tire marks."

"It looks far more premeditated in any case."

"The blow might have been struck in anger. Maybe whoever dumped him in the river did not realize he was still alive."

The medical examiner was even more convinced that Madeline and Stanley had been struck by a similar object, if not the same one.

"A baseball bat?"

"He doesn't rule it out."

Waring eventually responded to Philip's suggestion that he check out Hadley's whereabouts on the afternoon that Stanley Rune had been bludgeoned. He had told the detective of the Louisville Slugger Hadley had tried to use on him. "He had provocation, I grant you that. But that is still a pretty violent way to deal with someone snooping around your desk. And it suggests a modus operandi."

"Look, we had a motive for Hadley in the case of Madeline, or thought we did—younger man rebuffed by older woman for whom he has conceived a passion. Then we built a pretty good case against Stanley. What are you suggesting now, a chain re-action? Hadley kills Stanley because Stanley killed Madeline?"

"I don't know. Why don't we just find out where he was at the time? And why don't you get a warrant and confiscate his Louisville Slugger?"

"Anything else?"

Phil laughed. "I'm sorry. I'm more caught up in this than I thought. Menucci came to see me. He wants to hire me."

"Did you accept?"

"And have you run me off the reservation? No. I told him his interests were best served by the professional investigation that was being conducted by the police."

"What did he expect you to do?"

"What I'm already doing, I guess. Butting in. But I have no client."

When he got back to the apartment, Roger was not yet home but there was a young lady waiting in the lobby of the building.

"Do you remember me? Katherine George?"

And then he recognized the young graduate student who lived in the apartment over the garage at Bourke house.

"Roger should be home soon if you'd care to wait."

"Actually, it's you I should talk to."

"Come in."

She refused a soda, but Phil opened a beer, hoping that if he relaxed she would. She sat on the edge of her chair and seemed to be communing with herself as she looked at him.

"Can this be in confidence?"

"If it isn't a crime."

"But I think it might be."

"One you committed?"

"Oh no, of course not."

"Very well. Do you have a dollar?"

"What for?"

"You can hire me and then you can count on my confidentiality on everything that doesn't concern a crime."

"Well, then there's no point in that."

"I think you want to tell me anyway."

"I do." She took a deep breath and squared her shoulders. "I think I know who killed Mr. and Mrs. Rune."

"Tell me."

"I didn't see it happen, of course, but I am sure I know he did it."

"Who?"

She hesitated. "Promise me that if you think I'm crazy you'll tell me."

"I promise," he said, not smiling.

"I think it was Henry Hadley."

"Why?"

Henry had given her a big rush in recent months and she had been flattered; after all he was on the faculty, and he was single and settled so if anything developed, well, why not? She wasn't sure anything would develop, on her side, because she was never really sure that she liked him, but, still, you never know.

"And then I began to think he didn't really like me either. There was something else that explained his interest." She inhaled. "Where I live."

"At the Bourke house."

"Yes. Whenever he came to see me, he couldn't keep his mind off the main house. Or her."

"Mrs. Rune?"

"He was obsessed with her. I couldn't believe it at first, given his age and hers, but then there is some difference between his age and mine. Still, she was *old*."

"Comparatively speaking."

"You know what I mean."

"All too well." He thought of Janet Blair in Chicago, but of course she was older than Katherine George.

When Hadley insisted on going back to her place after the post-game party, she was concerned. He hadn't been drinking much and he had always been a gentleman before. "Too much of a gentleman, I see now. He wasn't really attracted to me." So she hadn't been too worried about letting him come up for a while when he brought her home, and they talked about this and that.

"About your brother, as a matter of fact. Henry resents the admiration I feel for Professor Knight."

It occurred to her later that he had left her place and been on the property around the time of Mrs. Rune's death. That hadn't meant anything to her right away, given how he felt about the woman. He could hardly kill the woman he was obsessed with.

"That's what I thought, anyway. He was on the property Friday afternoon too."

"Visiting you?"

"No. I had gotten up from my desk to pour some coffee and I went to the window to look out at the river. I saw him below, on the path that runs along the river."

"Walking?"

"Yes."

"In which direction?"

"South."

Away from where Stanley Rune's body was found. "Was he carrying anything."

She pursed her lips and her eyes widened. Then she nodded. "Yes. A kind of hiking staff."

25

Roger was driven home from the library by Greg Whelan in the archivist's car, which Roger likened to riding in the sidecar of a motorcycle. The front passenger seat was pushed forward until it pressed against the windshield and Roger had been wedged into the back seat through the single side door. "The way up and the way down may be the same way for Heraclitus," Roger observed, "but the sage was silent about the way in and the way out." He made this observation after Whelan had gone inside to enlist Philip's aid in extricating Roger and emerged with Katherine George as well.

She was needed as more than observer. She was able to slip in behind the driver's seat and push while Philip pulled until, with a pop, Roger was ejected from the car.

"I hope I haven't broken anything," the ponderous professor said.

"Where do you hurt?" Phil asked anxiously.

Greg cried, "I have insurance."

"I didn't mean me, I meant the car. Will your insurance cover damage incurred from doing a good deed? The van is in the library parking lot, Phil."

"I'll go over and pick it up later."

Phil helped Greg restore his car to its usual operating condition and the three of them waved the archivist on his way. At that point it occurred to Roger to wonder what Katherine was doing there.

"Come inside and I will tell you," Phil said.

"I hope you won't take this amiss if I say that this comes as a relief to me, Katherine," Roger said, after he had heard what his student had come to say. "When I first saw you and Henry together I must say that my reaction was one of astonishment. That he might be attracted to you was one thing. . . ."

"But he wasn't. He was using me."

Roger seemed to be seeking a way of saying that Katherine was better off being callously used by Henry Hadley than being loved by him, but such subtleties of the emotional order were not Roger's long suit and he wisely left well enough alone.

"On both occasions, he is at the scene of the crime. The first time, but for your sense of how it really stood between the two of you, might seem mere happenstance. The second time, would be the wildest coincidence. He has opportunity. Motive? I dislike seeing murders pile up like cars on a foggy California freeway, but my likes and dislikes are not criteria of likelihood. But why seek a separate killer for Madeline? The motives would have to differ. Thwarted passion in the one case?" Roger rubbed his face with both hands. "Why do I find it so difficult to see Henry in such a tragicomic role? Now why does he kill Stanley?"

"If Stanley was not responsible for Madeline's death?"

"Yes."

"Oh, he hated him," Katherine put in. "Only later did I wonder at his anger that Madeline should continue to see her life only in connection with Stanley. Separation and impending divorce meant nothing to her. She and Stanley were married once and for all, as long as they both should live. I said that I found that wonderful, and he wouldn't talk to me for fifteen minutes."

"Jealousy."

Waring arrived and it all had to be gone through again. "Are you game for a trip to Niles?" he asked Philip.

"I would never turn down an opportunity to visit Aunt Imogene. Did you take possession of his Louisville Slugger?"

Waring put his hand inside his jacket and drew into visibility a piece of paper, then put it back. "The warrant."

Katherine began to cry. "He's going to hate me so when he finds out what I've told you."

"You would have been in danger knowing what you did and not saying anything," Waring assured her, and her eyes rounded as she grasped the point of his remark.

Phil made arrangements for Waring to take him to the library parking lot where he would fetch the van and bring it back to the apartment. Then he and the lieutenant would go on to Niles and the confrontation with Henry Hadley.

At the door, Waring stopped and looked back at Roger. "A strange thing. The room clerk at the Evergreen Inn, the one who was on duty last Saturday night? He called to tell me that the cleaning ladies recognized the picture of Pamela Menucci in the paper. She was at the Evergreen that night, in the room rented by Stanley."

"But it wasn't Stanley who came for the key. Did he go up to the room?"

"The clerk doesn't know. He went back to reading Willa Cather after he gave the man a key."

"Have you asked Pamela about this yet?"

"I'm trying to figure out what to ask her. I don't want her father mad at me."

"How about some dinner?" Roger asked Katherine when Phil and Waring had gone.

"Do you cook?"

"After a fashion. I will make a risotto, you will make a salad, and I will make imitation garlic bread."

"How do you do that?"

On toast hot from the toaster, Roger spread butter liberally and then sprinkled the surface with garlic salt. No Italian restaurant would dare serve such a substitute, but, then, Roger was not going for a *cordon bleu*. Katherine's salad had so many ingredients, Roger had to look for the lettuce. The risotto was also loaded with goodies—mushrooms, tomato sauce, chopped onion, and green peas. Roger poured a glass of Phil's red wine for Katherine and for himself a large glass of ice water. When all was ready, he wheeled up to the table, bowed his head, and said grace.

"At home we only say grace at Thanksgiving."

"Meant to cover the whole year?"

"I never thought of it that way."

After they had eaten, he shook his head when Katherine began to talk again of the dreadful happenings of recent weeks.

"One, it is best to let these things seep down into the deeper recesses of the mind. Two, there is *Monday Night Football*. I assume you are a fan."

"Hey, I was an undergraduate here too, you know."

"We'll see how many former Notre Dame

players you can identify on the teams playing tonight. Can you wait until halftime for
popcorn?"

"Popcorn!"

"There's beer in the fridge."

"Would you like one?"

"I never take alcohol."

If she had asked, he could have given
half a dozen reasons for his abstemious-
ness, but he would not have mentioned the
most fundamental reason of all. He and Phil
had lost their parents in an accident that
had been caused by the drunkenness of
another motorist. The logical link between
that fact and Roger's total abstinence
would have been difficult to establish. Perhaps the link wasn't logical at all, but somehow it all came together in Roger's mind; it
was a way of commemorating and mourning his parents.

"Do you know Pamela Menucci?"

"She's a fruitcake."

"How so?"

"My folks knew her mother and she
sounds like what Pamela will become.
Henry would get furious whenever her
name came up."

"Why?"

"Same reason as with Madeline Rune. How could either of them possibly see anything that wasn't contemptible in Stanley Rune? Pamela was trying out for ingenue and femme fatale and wronged woman and half a dozen other parts as well. To say that she dramatizes things would be like saying that Joe Montana throws the ball."

The ball was thrown at that moment and, if not by Montana, by a pretty good quarterback, and the three monkeys of ABC Sports jabbered away simultaneously, ignored by Roger as he watched the receiver maneuver down the field, eluding tacklers, to cross the goal line.

"Touchdown!" Roger cried, lifting from his chair. "Let's put on the popcorn now."

26

Jack Buck and Hank Stram dominated the conversation as Phil and Waring drove up Route 33 to Niles.

"Sorry about that," Waring said. "I forgot about *Monday Night Football.*"

"I prefer it on radio. Often we cut the sound of the TV and listen to these two. They tend to watch the game."

The touchdown that had elated Roger in South Bend elated Phil just as they crossed the Michigan line. Waring was guided by Phil, who had been to the house before.

"And nearly got brained."

"First thing we do is confiscate that bat."

To the naked eye, there had been nothing to indicate that Hadley's Louisville Slugger had been the weapon with which Madeline Rune had been struck. But careful laboratory examination might prove otherwise. Pulchrasky and her crew were searching along the riverbank to see if they could find what Katherine had described as a hiking staff.

It was a bit of a surprise, when they got to the house, to find that Imogene had the game on. Indeed, she had it on so loud that the doorbell was inaudible to her. Phil went along the porch and tapped on the window with his keys. Imogene spun around, frightened, and he put his face close to the window, so she could see who he was. She screamed so loudly it carried over the sound of the television. Her terrified gaze turned to the door. Apparently she had picked up the sound of Waring's thunderous pounding on the front door. Phil kept his face visible, hoping for recognition, and then, thank God, it came. She leaned forward and peered at him. He smiled reassuringly and pointed toward the door.

"You scared me half to death," Imogene

chided, when she had let them in. "You're from South Bend?" she asked Waring.

"That's right. Is your nephew home?"

"What do you want?" It was the voice of Henry Hadley, and the sound of it behind him made Phil wheel to face him.

Waring said, "I want to talk to you."

"You didn't have to beat the door down."

"Where can we talk?"

Hadley hesitated. Did he suspect why they were here and did not want his aunt disturbed by their questions? In any case, he invited them down to his lair. The roar of Imogene's television followed them to the stairway but was muffled when that door was pulled shut behind them. In the basement, however, the exposed boards seemed to reverberate with the sound from above. In Hadley's enclosed apartment, with its acoustic ceiling, it was almost peaceful.

"I'm sick of football," he said, but neither of his visitors commented on this character flaw.

"Stanley Rune has been killed," Waring noted.

"I heard."

"First Madeline, now Stanley."

Hadley shook his head. "South Bend is becoming a dangerous place to live."

"I want to review with you what you have already told us, if you don't mind."

"What are you looking for?" Hadley asked Phil, who had begun to search for the bat.

"Your Louisville Slugger."

"My what?"

"Your baseball bat."

"I don't have a baseball bat."

"Come on, Henry. You tried to clobber me with it the last time I was here."

Phil had reached a closet and his hand was on the door when Henry flew across the room and jerked Phil's hand away from the knob. Waring was right behind Henry and got his arms around him, pulling him away from Phil. Hadley struggled in Waring's arms while Phil pulled open the closet door. He pulled a string that turned on a light and then Hadley broke free and pushed Phil forward into the closet and then began to grope around in a corner. In a moment, Hadley turned, a strange expression on his face.

"Nice going," he said to Waring with disgust, and went back across the room to his workspace.

"What do you mean?"

"When did you break in here and take it?"

"Take what?"

"The goddam bat. Don't try to argue that my effort to protect my property means anything else but that. You come in, start rummaging around in my closet. . . ."

"I have a warrant to search this place, Henry." Waring brought it out, but Henry had no interest in seeing it. "This is Niles, Detective. What good is that here?"

Waring explained the cooperation with the Niles police and the fact that the warrant was from a Michigan judge, but Henry's disinterest only increased. Watching all this, Phil wondered how cagey Henry Hadley was. First he had denied he owned a bat and then when the search for it began he put on a great act of preventing its being found. Now he was accusing Waring of having already confiscated it surreptitiously. Either the bat was on the premises, and the fiasco at the closet was merely meant to deter any further search, or the bat really was gone, and since the police did not have it that meant Hadley had gotten rid of it. Phil continued to search for the bat while Waring talked to Hadley.

"You were at the Bourke house the night, or rather morning, Madeline Rune was killed."

"I was in the apartment over the garage, yes."

"And you left about three o'clock."

"Did I? I don't remember."

"The girl does."

"Katherine?"

"She also remembers seeing you on the river path last Friday at about the time Stanley Rune was killed."

"Carrying a baseball bat?"

"Is that what you used on Madeline?"

"Hey, what is this? Shouldn't I have a lawyer?"

"I think you better."

Hadley stared at Waring. "You're serious."

"Call your lawyer."

"I don't have a lawyer."

"Try the Yellow Pages."

Meanwhile, Waring called the Niles department and five minutes later a patrol car came, disturbing Imogene once again.

"You're lucky it's halftime," she told the officers, as she pointed them toward the stairway. She turned to Phil, "What's going on?"

"They think Henry had something to do with the deaths of Madeline and Stanley Rune."

She thought about it. "You mean killed them?"

"I'm sorry about this, Miss Hadley. It looks bad, but you never know."

"Oh, he could have done it, no doubt about that. He has a lot of the other side of the family in him."

It seemed a shame that Henry didn't even have his family in his corner. The second half began as they were taking Henry away.

"Did you turn off the lights down there, Henry?" Imogene asked.

He stopped and looked at her. "How would you know whether they're on or off?"

"When the bills come."

It was an odd farewell, but on that note

Henry was taken out to Waring's car and put into the back seat. Phil got into the passenger seat and turned to face Henry.

"You don't mind if we listen to the game, do you, Henry?"

"Would it matter?"

"It will be better if you don't say anything until you have a lawyer."

Waring had just pulled open the driver's door when Henry leaned forward and asked Phil, "Do you really think I killed those people?"

"We'll see."

"Tell me what you think!"

"Better cool it, Hadley."

The motor went on and with it the radio and Hadley threw himself against the back of the seat, disgusted. Phil was glad not to have to answer the question. The fact is he had thought Stanley Rune killed Madeline, and of course that was still possible, but the case against Henry almost required that he had killed the both of them. His presence on the river path last Friday was a pretty flimsy basis to link him to the death of Stanley. Of course there was all they had learned about Henry's attitude toward the husband of

Madeline Rune. Would Katherine be as willing to say in court what she had said to Roger?

And where was the Louisville Slugger?

27

In the Corby Hall dining room, discussion of the murder first of a university trustee and then of her estranged husband prompted remarks ranging from the rueful through the callous to the philosophical.

"I knew her father, wonderful man."

"A Bourke."

"The son of F. X."

"He died in Korea."

"Is that the end of the Bourkes?"

"Is it true the name was originally Borkowski?"

"No! F. X. was Irish through and through."

"Jameson?"

"That too. Proof positive."

"Hundred proof."

"Did you know that F. X. wrote a series of boys' books under a pen name?"

If anyone at the senior table knew this, they gave no indication. Nor with the wisdom of years did they indicate that they did not know something Carmody did.

"Did we know or did he write them?" Reith asked, smiling slyly.

At the Old Bastards table in the University Club, the conversation went back and forth between the two games already played and the home game coming up on Saturday.

"I'm worried."

"We're favored by three touchdowns."

"That's the kind you lose."

"Not at home."

"Anyone else killed lately?"

"I guess they took the body of the husband to Chicago for burial."

"Wasn't he a Domer?"

"A double Domer. He married one."

"An incestuous union."

"They seldom work out."

"They arrested Hadley."

"What's the motive?"

"An incestuous union."

In the archives, Greg Walsh sat by the window in a workroom and looked out over the campus. The view from the sixth floor was in many ways better than that from the top floor. There the campus and buildings looked as they did from an airplane descending to the Michiana Airport, whose runway was just barely visible to Greg below the western horizon. The war memorial dominated the mall west of the library, rising like Stonehenge from its marble base, with fountains spouting randomly among the roughhewn pillars. An anonymous tribute to the alumni who had served in the past three wars, World War II, the Korean conflict, and, despite predictable protests at the time the monument went up, Vietnam. How the scale of the place had changed since two plaques flanking the east door of Sacred Heart had sufficed to name all those who had fallen in World War I. For God, Country and Notre Dame. And on the right-hand plaque the name of the man to whom Rockne had dedicated the book that so fascinated Roger Knight. Arnold J. Mc-

Inerny. Greg had run a check on the man. No surprises.

Lenore had made no progress at all in discovering when and how the Bourke papers were to be turned over. Manfred Dosch, who had been hired by Stanley Rune when he was accused of killing his wife, had been asked by the Walkers to look after the family interests.

"The Walkers?" the chief archivist asked.

"I believe they are cousins of a sort," Dosch said.

"I never heard the name mentioned before," Lenore said. Her expression suggested that to be was to be perceived by her.

"Mrs. Walker was married to a cousin of Madeline."

"Was?"

"He died and she married again."

"What kind of cousin is that?"

She was even less pleased when she learned that it had been this same Mrs. Walker who had tried to persuade Madeline to renege on the gift of F. X. Bourke's papers to Notre Dame and to turn the family house into a museum. She and Mr. Walker had volunteered to act as live-in caretakers.

"No wonder they're stonewalling," she observed to Roger.

"Well, Stanley was only buried two days ago," he said.

But if Roger Knight thus tried to mollify the chief archivist, in conversation with Greg Walsh he indicated his own forebodings about the Walkers. They might be able to persuade Manfred Dosch to adopt their point of view.

"The fact that the papers have not been turned over for so many years may constitute some legal basis for rejecting that provision of the will."

"Isn't there any money involved? You'd think they'd be more interested in that. Has either one of the Walkers any museum experience?"

"I think he was a librarian."

"Is there any money?"

"Good question."

Mario Miranda thought it was a good question too. The university counsel had shown exceptional patience in the matter of the F. X. Bourke papers, perhaps taking his cue from the administration which, no longer able to contain the sensational coverage of the deaths of Madeline and Stanley Rune, with the mandatory mention in any story of the Notre Dame connection, had returned to its policy of downplaying the athletic facet of the university's greatness. But the mention of money prompted Miranda to call for the Bourke file and soon he had a copy of F. X.'s will on the desk before him.

"Give me a minute," he said to Roger Knight.

"Take your time."

But Miranda was already lost in the mesmerizing prose of the document before him, written by the legendary Alexis Cholis, who had claimed kinship with the Coquillards, who had been among the founders of South Bend, as well as with the Miami tribe the government had driven from this place into the southwestern United States. In the hands of Cholis, the English language shed a century or two. Eighteenth-century periodic sentences, sprouting clauses and sub-phrases as they spread across the page, required just the kind of undivided attention Mario Miranda was giving the product of the pen of Alexis Cholis.

"If there is any money, the university gets half," he said, looking up.

"That sounds like an interest."

"I'm not through. He might take it all back before he finishes."

The "he" in question was clearly Cholis, not F. X. Bourke. Miranda's office was in the Main Building, under the golden dome from which the Blessed Virgin Mary looks ever southward, as if recalling the years that Father Sorin spent in Vincennes before coming north in 1842 and taking possession of this land surrounding the twin lakes of St. Mary and St. Joseph. French missionaries had worked here two centuries earlier and the redoubtable Badin, the first priest ordained in the United States, was the missionary from whom Sorin bought the land. Badin lay buried now in the log chapel, the oldest campus building, in which small weddings and special liturgies were held. The building in which Mario Miranda read the will of F. X. Bourke was one that went back to Sorin himself, built hastily after an 1879 fire had leveled its predecessor. Roger had seen photographs of Sorin sitting bearded and patriarchal among the visiting prelates who had been in attendance for the golden anniversary celebration and the backdrop had been this building. It had been remodeled many times and its various floors and wings put to a multiplicity of uses over the years, but still it was the same building.

"You must derive a great deal of satisfaction from having your office in this building."

"This has always been the university counsel's office. They wanted me to move."

"And you refused?"

"No. They changed their mind."

It was difficult to know what made Miranda tick. The general rule was, scratch a student or professor or administrator and you would discover beneath whatever exterior a fanatic and sentimental lover of Notre Dame. Miranda pretended to be, or perhaps just was, a complete functionary. Only the mention of possible money in the Bourke bequest had triggered anything like enthusiasm.

He sat back. "It stands. We get half."

"Of what?"

"That is the question. I'll get in touch with Dosch. Thanks for stopping by, Professor."

"This could be an effective lever to have

those papers released to the university archives, don't you think?"

"Do they have room for them?"

This raised a question that the archivist would pursue. Back in the apartment, having driven in his golf cart from the Main Building to the Hesburgh Center, Roger telephoned Marcus Bramble at the number where the donor could always be reached.

"If I don't answer that number, call the police."

The phone was answered on the first ring. "Yeah?"

"This is Roger Knight, Marcus."

"Roger! I was just talking about you."

"But I've never played football."

"Ho ho. Too bad. You'd make the Refrigerator look like a picnic cooler. No, I'm talking with a Mrs. Walker, who has a very interesting proposition. I'd like to have you in on the discussion."

"Are you coming for the game Saturday?"

"Are you kidding? Of course I'm coming. Let's sit together."

"My brother and I have seats under the press box."

"Under the press box! That's no good. Join my party, I have some extra tickets."

"We can talk about that interesting proposition then."

Bramble asked Mrs. Walker if she would be in South Bend for the weekend and conveyed to Roger her willingness to join them.

After he hung up, Roger sat back and thought of how strong a hand the Walkers would have if they enlisted Marcus Bramble in their effort. He picked up the phone and put through a call to Miranda to tell him of this development. That done, he pushed away from his desk, plucked a William X. McNaughton novel from the coffee table, and settled himself in the natural light from the window to continue reading *The Losing Season*.

28

Father Quirk, usually so equanimous, reacted with excited anger to the news that a glitch had developed in the transfer of the F. X. Bourke papers to the university archives. Roger and Father Carmody had stopped by to share this news.

"That was his explicit wish! I know. I was with him at the end."

It took an effort to imagine Quirk as a young priest, performing pastoral tasks.

"Oh, it's in his will as well," Roger said.

"Those papers are much more important than the money."

"Was he a wealthy man?"

"Wealthy?" Quirk's cadaverous countenance assumed an expression of amasement. "He had the Midas touch. His column was syndicated across the nation. And of course he made a bundle from those boys' books. He always claimed to have given Rock the idea for *The Four Winners.*"

Roger knew that Rockne had been an irrepressible risk taker, always on the alert for a money-making scheme. In this as in much else, he was far in advance of his fellow coaches and would have competed well with some of the entrepreneurial wizards now at the head of college coaching staffs. Rockne had spent an hour with his broker every morning; his summer camps had provided employment for his athletes and other students as well as added income to the coach. His book on coaching had known a vast success. It was entirely plausible that, seeing how his old teammate was earning impressive sums writing stories of prep school football, he decided to try a hand at it himself.

"I'm afraid he lacked F. X. Bourke's— should I say William X. McNaughton's?— storytelling gifts."

"F. X. offered to help him, but he bristled

at the idea that he couldn't do the thing himself."

"I thought you said he did get help from Bourke."

"Oh, he gave in eventually. That book was the hardest thing he ever did."

"And you typed it?"

"First what the Rock did. Then I handed it on to Bourke."

"It will be a fascinating project to compare Rockne's draft with the Bourke version."

"Why don't you get that Bramble fellow to go after those papers? He sounds like a man who gets things done."

Roger decided not to tell Father Quirk that the Walkers had already contacted the donor and that Bramble had sounded amenable to their scheme.

He said, "Mr. Bramble will be here Saturday for the game."

"I hope he comes to see me."

"I don't think he could be kept away."

Roger took Father Carmody back to the campus in his golf cart. The priest had had little to say during the visit to Father Quirk at Holy Cross House.

"I suppose it seems silly to talk about sports at a time like this," Roger said.

"What do you mean?"

"Stanley Rune."

"What happened to him?" Father Carmody asked the question with alarm.

"Father, you must have heard."

Carmody thought about it. "If I did I've forgotten."

"He's dead."

"Who?"

"Stanley Rune."

"You mean his wife."

"Her too."

"I remember that," Father Carmody said with some satisfaction. Roger let it go. It was sad to realize that the time was not far distant when Father Carmody would be taking up permanent residence at Holy Cross Hall.

There was a message from Marcus Bramble, and when Roger called the wealthy alumnus he said that he had been thinking.

"What would you say of turning the Bourke mansion into the Rockne memorial? He could be reburied there on the grounds, maybe in a mausoleum, but we could discuss that. Inside, we would redesign the place, but respecting the original purpose of the rooms."

Bramble went on and Roger listened with sinking heart. It sounded as if the Walkers had made their case already and that waiting for the weekend had been a mistake.

"Marcus, there are several houses in South Bend that Rockne himself actually lived in. One is on St. Vincent Avenue, just a short walk from campus. As long as you're turning over this idea, you might add those houses to the mix. That would preserve the Notre Dame connection."

"How could anything involving Rockne not connect to Notre Dame?"

"The memorial would no longer be something on campus."

A silence. "That's true."

"And since the F. X. Bourke papers will come to Notre Dame, the question would arise why Rockne is being memorialized in Bourke's house when Bourke's stuff is on campus."

"You don't like the idea."

"It sounds like something some people in the administration would want you to do."

"How do you mean?"

"You must have noticed that the reaction to your offer of ten million dollars for a Rockne memorial has been lukewarm."

"I did expect more enthusiasm."

"There are some who might take it as a victory of sorts if you should transfer your idea off-campus."

"I wish I had talked with you earlier."

"We can talk when you're here for the game."

"I'm looking forward to that." And then, in a switch of topic, "I never did think Stanley Rune killed his wife."

"But you were the one who said she had been threatened by him."

"That's why he couldn't have done it. People who threaten things don't do them, in my experience. If someone tells you he is going to sue you, chances are he won't."

"A young man named Henry Hadley has been arrested."

"It said on TV that he is a member of the faculty."

"That's right."

And that is why Roger's suggestion that there were those in the administration who might welcome the relocation of Marcus

Bramble's Knute Rockne memorial was less than candid. Madeline Rune's connection to the university had been real, and by a legitimate extension her husband's death too was regarded as in some way a university matter, but to have a member of the faculty charged with their deaths was undeniably very very bad publicity for Notre Dame.

In the faculty senate a debate raged as to whether the faculty as a whole should undertake to pay the legal expenses of Henry Hadley.

"I second the motion," Basquette said, and everyone turned to look at him. He grinned and added, "I in turn move that we undertake to pay the funeral expenses of Madeline and Stanley Rune."

"Don't be absurd."

"I couldn't put it better myself."

Fondus rose to say that she agreed entirely with Basquette. It was absurd to ask the faculty to shoulder such an expense. "Surely this is something the university as such should do."

"It ought to be a fringe benefit," Basquette said. "Legal representation whenever accused of a capital crime."

"Oh, shut up."

"Who is Hadley anyway?"

"He teaches comic books."

"Is that a graduate course?"

The president gaveled the meeting into a semblance of order. He thought their time might be profitably spent looking into the hiring of Henry Hadley.

"I received an anonymous e-mail suggesting that the procedure was irregular."

"Is *MAD* magazine discussed in his course?"

But Basquette had received all the attention he was going to receive that night. The grievances of the faculty were the fuel of the senate and the body could not take lightly the taking lightly of them. A serious and sober discussion ensued, which would be duly reported to the faculty, printed, and distributed, lest any sweetness be wasted only in the desert air of the faculty senate.

29

A Louisville Slugger was found in the trunk of Henry Hadley's car and Mrs. Walker turned over to the police some curious documents she found in the bedroom of her late cousin.

"At how many removes?" Roger asked, irked to learn that the Walkers had apparently taken possession of the Bourke house.

"Definitively removed now."

The documents were letters to Madeline from Hadley and, according to Waring, were pretty routine stuff, except for one.

"He threatened her. If he couldn't have her no one would."

"Are they all written in the same hand?" Phil asked.

"They were written on a computer and printed out."

Roger said, "Nobody writes letters anymore. Any project to compile a person's letters from now on will consist of retrieving things from hard disks."

"You should talk."

"I didn't mean it as an accusation. One might as well get nostalgic over clay tablets as over the thought of people seated at their writing desks all morning answering their correspondence. I have made my peace with e-mail."

"Did Madeline have a computer?"

"The latest thing. You can think of her as seated at her keyboard all morning sending and answering e-mail messages."

"It would be very interesting to see her computer," Roger said, looking hopefully at Waring.

"Just out of curiosity?"

"At least that. Could you get me past the Walkers?"

"What do you mean?"

"The fact that she was snooping around Madeline's room suggests that she has taken over the house."

"Ha! Mrs. Taylor is on guard and she doesn't like the Walkers at all. I gave Mrs. Walker two hours in the house, accompanied by Edna Pulchrasky. Manfred Dosch was there too."

Waring promised to have Edna on duty that afternoon so that Whelan could drive him up in the van and they could check out Madeline's computer.

"I'll give you equal time. Two hours."

"Fair enough. It will be good to meet Mrs. Taylor."

"I thought you had been to the house before."

"She is a dubious watchdog, Waring. As far as I know, we came and went without her knowledge. But there was the sound of television from her room on the third floor."

"Well, she was on duty while Mrs. Walker was in the house."

A call came from Marcus Bramble not long after Waring had left.

"I just got in. Your brother there?" Bramble asked without ceremony.

Roger passed the phone to Phil, who perked up as he listened. "I'm on my way," he said, rising to his feet before hanging up. "An invitation to golf," he said to Roger.

"Wonderful."

While Phil readied himself for the links, Roger got in touch with Mario Miranda, the university counsel.

"Have the police been keeping you informed on the Henry Hadley investigation?"

Miranda moaned. "What weeks these have been." He was mourning the university's reputation rather than the deaths of the Runes or the impending trial of Henry Hadley for double murder. Then his tone changed. "Has something come up?"

"Not good news, I'm afraid. They have found what look to be incriminating messages from Hadley in Madeline Rune's room."

"I hope they nail that sonofagun and quick."

"I would very much like to have access to Hadley's campus office. Have the police sealed it off?"

"No! It's locked and secure enough with-

out them stringing yellow tape all over Decio."

Decio was the trinity of joined narrow
structures north of the stadium that housed
the faculty.

"Then you could let me in."

"Will this expedite the investigation?"

Roger did not like to leave Miranda with
the impression that he was eagerly looking
for more rope with which to hang Henry
Hadley, but if that is what a search of Hadley's computer produced, it would come to
light sooner or later anyway. Miranda arranged to meet Roger at Decio and ten
minutes later, having waved Phil off to his
golf match with Marcus Bramble, Roger got
himself into his golf cart and moved silently
along the diagonal walkways toward Decio.

As had been the case two weeks before,
the campus was already crowded with visitors here for the game. The weather could
not have been a better example of autum-
nal beauty in northern Indiana. There was
a crispness in the air and the leaves were
just beginning to turn. Here and there, a
dogwood gleamed redly in the autumn air.
Roger's progress was desultory, as he had
to maneuver around pedestrians and some-

times simply slow to a crawl. He hated to sound a warning, and the cart was so quiet that people often jumped when they turned to see it at their heels and the massive, smiling Roger behind the wheel.

"Toot toot," he said when this happened and was allowed to proceed.

As he neared Decio, he saw Miranda coming to meet him on the walkway, his hands raised. He hopped onto what was left of the front seat and leaned toward Roger.

"Pull over there by that side door. I don't want to draw attention to this."

"The emergency exit?"

"It's okay. I had them deactivate it. This way we can slip in unnoticed. Hadley's office is only four doors from this entrance."

Roger parked and joined Miranda at the emergency door. The university counsel put in a key, turned it, and pulled the door open. A horrendous clanging noise began and the panicky Miranda seemed unsure whether to go or stay. Finally he took Roger's arm and pulled him through the door, pulling it shut behind them. But closing the door did not make the alarm cease. Miranda scurried down the hall to an office, inserted another key and disappeared inside. By the time Roger got there, the hallway was filled with faculty.

"Is it a fire?"

"What's going on?"

"A student must have done it."

Roger nodded, sharing their amazement and backed into Hadley's office. Miranda shut the door and looked at him.

"This better be important."

"Are you going to wait?"

"What do you mean?"

"The door will lock when I close it. There's no need for you to waste time here."

The thought of escape clearly appealed to Miranda. "I'll wait until things quiet down."

Even as he spoke, the alarm stopped and the ensuing silence was almost palpable.

"My God, what a racket," Miranda said.

"It's pretty hard to ignore."

"Wait until I get my hands on Whipple."

Whipple apparently was the security man who had promised to deactivate the alarm. When Miranda slipped out of the office ten minutes later, Roger scarcely noticed. He tapped into Eudora and brought up Hadley's e-mail, but a dialogue box asked for a password. Without the password, it would be impossible to go further and this visit would be a waste of time. Roger shut his eyes and imagined that he was Henry Hadley choosing a password. He let his mind fill with the image of the scruffy assistant professor; he thought of him as infatuated with Madeline Rune; he remembered him in the archives. Roger's eyes opened and he looked at the blank in the dialogue box waiting to have Hadley's password entered. Suddenly he smiled and began to type. ROCKNE. Bingo! He had access to Hadley's e-mail. No chime went off indicating new and unread mail. Roger opened the file of messages sent and, scrolling through it, could see the number of messages Hadley had sent to Madeline in care of an America Online address.

Reading them, he wondered what the police would make of them. By and large, they were innocuous, requesting Madeline's support for the novel he was writing, requesting access to the study of F. X. Bourke. He pleaded with her to see his debunking novel as supportive of the ideals for which her grandfather had stood. He appealed to her as someone like herself, whose roots went deep into the past of Notre Dame.

"My aim is to help Notre Dame," he professed.

In reply, Madeline said that she understood his pain but did not see a cure. Her replies—and they were always just responses to his messages—crisp, short, to the point, seemed to seek a telegraphic parsimony.

Roger printed out both ends of the exchange, wanting the complement to what had been provided to the police. Or at least of most of what had been provided Waring.

He picked up the phone, intending to call Greg Whelan to ask the archivist to meet him at Decio so they could ride back together to the golf cart, when he noticed the call-waiting button on. He punched the number that would enable him to hear the message and suddenly his ear was filled with an hysterical female voice.

"Leave me alone, leave me alone, if you don't stop this I am going to call the police. You're dangerous, do you know that? Violent! If you threaten me one more time. . . ."

Her voice ran out of control and then she was out of air and the message stopped.

For fifteen minutes, Roger sat on in Henry Hadley's office, his hands flat on the desk before him, eyes closed, just thinking, letting the thoughts come, not forcing them in this direction or that. And then he called Greg Whelan.

Mrs. Taylor was struck dumb by the size of Roger Knight and this made her more than amenable to his requests.

"Is that a special vehicle?" she asked, looking out at the van.

"Remodeled just for me."

"Do you remember *Ironsides*?"

"The ship?"

She shook her head. "The television show. He had a truck like that."

"This is Greg Walsh, an archivist at Notre Dame."

"What in the world is that?"

"You may well ask. He collects things."

"I'll keep an eye on him."

"Good idea. You've been having a lot of visitors lately, haven't you?"

"Since poor Maddie's death, it's been a circus. Then him too." She shook her head.

"People wonder why I stay? I could be next." Her eyes grew great with the significance of her remark.

"Henry Hadley is in jail," Edna Pulchrasky assured the elderly woman.

"What a strange bird that one is."

"Was Mrs. Rune frightened of him?"

"That little runt? He was a pest, I can tell you that. He just wouldn't leave her alone."

They had wandered inside during this exchange. Mrs. Taylor said they could just go up by themselves, as she wasn't going to climb those stairs again until she had to.

"Do you think you should?" she asked Roger.

Roger laughed at her concern but he was puffing before he reached the landing, and Greg Whelan and Edna Pulchraski each took an arm and pulled him up the rest of the way. Edna showed the way to Madeline's room.

In what had been designed originally as a sitting room off her bedroom, Madeline had created a very nice workspace. Her electronic equipment was the last word and yet it seemed almost unobtrusive. A mini-tower was concealed beneath the table, the monitor and keyboard shared the surface with a scanner and printer. A screensaver undulated on the monitor screen.

"Did you leave it on?" Roger asked Edna.

"I guess she never turned it off. According to Mrs. Taylor."

"There are two schools of thought on that," Roger murmured. Some said turning a computer on and off frequently was wearing, the alternate heat and cold aging the machine, while others pointed out the cost of electricity, adding that most computers were obsolete before they wore out. But perhaps Madeline had simply liked the mesmerizing presence of that constantly altering shape upon the screen.

After having examined Henry Hadley's computer, Roger found little new on Madeline's, at least on the topic that interested him. But the threatening note that had not been logged on messages sent on Henry's machine was on the screen when Roger put Eudora in the background and a word-processing program came on.

I am going to strike and strike again, nothing can stop me now. Everything depends on my success and I shall sweep aside

*anyone standing in my way. Today is the
day when my opponent is my enemy and
war has been declared.*

Roger struck a few keys and the printer began to hum.

"What are you doing?"

"Making a copy for myself. Okay?"

Edna shrugged.

When the message was printed, Roger
pushed back from the table and got to his
feet.

"Want to take a look at it, Greg?"

Standing behind the archivist, who un-
ashamedly examined file after file, Roger
could see that Madeline had been a good
manager of what had been left to her. One
spreadsheet indicated that the market
value of her stock was close to three million. Not exactly a Bramble-like sum but
sufficient to interest Mario Miranda.

Downstairs, Mrs. Taylor had made tea
and sandwiches and they all sat at the dining room table, Roger perched precariously
on the edge of a chair.

"You finished faster than the others."

"How long have you lived in this house,
Mrs. Taylor?"

"Lived here? I'm just the housekeeper."

"You have the place to yourself now," Edna said.

"Oh, there were years when I was all alone, until Maddie moved back."

Edna went to answer the ringing phone, taking the call in the kitchen. The murmur of her voice was audible and then she returned and sat, her brows lifted.

"That was Detective Waring. The Louisville Slugger found in the trunk of Hadley's car? It was the murder weapon. Both times."

When Phil arrived at the South Bend Country Club, Marcus Bramble was waiting impatiently.

"I tried to make up a foursome, but no luck."

"Good. Fewer witnesses."

"What's your handicap?"

Bramble could not repress a smile when Phil told him. "How about a buck a hole?"

Phil was fitted out with appropriate toggery less gaudy than Bramble's and a set of clubs, and soon they purred down to the tenth tee in Bramble's cart. Phil went through the ritual of saying how long it had

been since he last golfed, he scarcely remembered how to do it, and the rest of the
litany. Bramble ignored this, teed up, and
skimmed the ball out 150 yards. Phil felt
considerably encouraged as he addressed
his own ball. He topped it and it trickled
down the hill, not reaching the fairway.

"Mulligan," Bramble said.

"I accept."

Phil teed up another ball, took his time,
tried to swing in slow motion, caught the
ball, and gave it a decent ride.

"Sandbagger," Bramble muttered when
Phil got beside him in the cart. He un-
wrapped a candy bar and bit off a third of
it. Phil declined the offer of a bite. It was
like being offered a wad of tobacco. "I'm
trying to cut down on food."

"With candy bars?"

"I skip lunch."

He also skipped counting a couple
strokes, but Phil, mindful of the Mulligan
granted him on the opening hole, decided
to play the course rather than his opponent.
Either way he would lose, but there is defeat and defeat. After nine holes, not even
the new math could disguise the fact that
Bramble was not playing well.

"I'm distracted. Mind if we call it quits?"

They showered and dressed and then sat on the veranda sipping gin and tonics. Phil brought Bramble up to speed on the Hadley investigation. He had called Roger from the locker room, not expecting to find him home, and had heard of the new developments. Bramble shook his head.

"And they said that the computer would spell the end of paper."

"A final message threatening her and a record of her hysterical voice telling him to leave her alone."

"If that happened before Saturday when I spent time with her at the bar of the Morris Inn, she certainly was handling it well."

"I don't know when these communications took place."

"Well, the sonofagun has sure taken the edge off my Rockne memorial offer."

"Hadley hated Rockne. Or at least, the part he plays in the Notre Dame mystique."

"Mystique?"

"Legend."

"That sounds like lies to me. What does he know about Rockne, anyway?"

Marcus Bramble himself had only a superficial knowledge of the life and times and activities of the great coach, but it was sufficient to enlist his undying admiration.

"I am going to have that museum, Phil. It is an idea whose time has come."

"On campus?"

Bramble's brow clouded. "That's another thing I mean to have cleared up this weekend."

"How do you think we'll do tomorrow?"

"We'll beat 'em. I don't care what the odds are."

The previous year's national champion was coming to South Bend, bringing a record identical to Notre Dame's, 2-0. Bramble's NFL team was also doing well, but at this point in the season it was difficult to get excited. Only a few teams would be kept out of the play-offs, given the wild card system, so the playing millionaires worked mainly at keeping their postseason chances alive, no great task.

"Going to the president's party tonight?"

"Roger and I plan on a quiet evening at home."

"I envy you. My life is spent bouncing from city to city. One of these days I am going to settle down."

"Stop by later if you'd like."

* * *

And he did stop by too, about one forty-five, banging on the door and announcing that it was Marcus Bramble come to party. They decided to ignore him. To open the door was to be involved in at least a fifteen-minute effort to persuade the diminutive donor to hit the sack.

Saturday morning was a dull, cloudy day, shades of gray, with a chill little wind nipping across the campus. If the fans noticed, they gave no sign of it. Bright eyed, rosy cheeked, bundled up against the cold, they wandered the campus, going from hall to hall, stopping for a grilled hamburger, adding the little puffs of their breathing to the smoke rising from the grills. The sound of the band was carried on the breeze, arriving in intermittent bursts as the wind rose and fell.

"Football weather," someone said.

"Notre Dame weather. Those kids from southern California can't stand it."

The drive in the golf cart from the Hesburgh Center was not long, but Roger and Phil took it in stages, from time to time stopping at a bench and breathing in the festive atmosphere.

"Do you know why they keep calling this place unique, Phil?"

"Why?"

"Because it's true."

If Roger had been asked to sign a long-term contract at that moment, he would not have hesitated. This is where he wanted to be for as long as might be, that was his feeling. Phil, of course, would think he meant football, and of course he did, but that was only a part of it, a small part, he could now see. His seminar had become more satisfying than he would have imag-ined, although he was startled by how little of the Catholic tradition his students seemed to know. Perhaps it should not have been surprising that Paul Claudel was less than a household name for them, but it was not only foreign authors who were foreign to them. One day, he mentioned Merton and had been interrupted by Kath-erine George, of all people.

"Who is Merton?"

"Thomas Merton?"

But no light of recognition came. Good

Lord. It was an unsettling realization that he, a convert, had a more extensive grasp of Catholic culture than these products, by and large, of a Catholic education. Somehow Catholic institutions had participated in the marginalizing of their own tradition, seeking to become indistinguishable from secular institutions. But nowadays that meant the denial of culture, not the switching from one to another. That the nihilism of many contemporary literary critics was represented at Notre Dame had come as a shock to Roger. He began to see the point of those who argued that the university was rapidly secularizing itself. And Roger also began to surmise the true significance of the Huneker Professorship of Catholic Studies. One of the attractions of staying would be to do missionary work among the supposedly saved.

From the bench on which they now sat they could see the band approaching from the Main Building, playing the fight song. They rose and continued on to the stadium. The half hour that yet remained before game time passed quickly as the stands filled; the opposing bands serenaded the opposition, playing the enemy's fight song.

Above the stadium, the Goodyear blimp came into view and the procession of small planes dragging banners behind. The captains met in midfield, the coin was tossed, and the umpire signaled the results. Notre Dame would kick off.

It was a high and perfect kick, the ball tumbling over and over as it described a high arc, arriving in the receiver's hands a second before the first wave of Notre Dame defenders. The ball was spotted on the 18. The first play was a fake run into the line with the quarterback dropping back in a perfect deception. Before the defending line grasped what had happened, he launched a forty-yard pass that was gathered in by the fleet receiver and carried into the end zone with no defender within five yards of him. The sky above the stadium seemed to grow darker as a silence fell.

But it was early. There was a whole game left to play. Notre Dame fans could admire a trick play once in a while, but the opponent would not be able to survive the afternoon without getting down to meat and potatoes. The fans had revived when Notre Dame grounded the kickoff in the end zone and began from the 20. Three plays had gained only seven yards, three runs that seemed to hit a stone wall. The punt was wobbly and unsure and barely crossed the mid-field mark. The first play from scrimmage had everyone on their edge of their seats—the students of course would stand throughout this game as they did every game. Again a fake into the line and what looked to be a fake hand-off as the quarterback dropped back. He was smothered under three charging defenders. But the hand-off had been genuine and the player with the ball was brought down by a desperation tackle that popped the ball loose into the end zone. The first player to reach it was a Notre Dame player, but when the pile of bodies was unpacked the man with the ball at the bottom did not wear a Notre Dame uniform. The opponent had run two plays and scored two touchdowns. It was difficult not to feel that divine favor had been withdrawn and the afternoon would be long and painful.

It was long, but there was no more scoring in the first half. As the teams trotted off the field, there was almost relief that things had not continued to go as they had in the first minutes. But the Notre Dame offense had continued to play an ineffective ground game. Marcus Bramble came up the stairs during the half, working against the flow of those going below for refreshments.

"Hey, I stopped by last night."

"You did! What time was that?"

"I'm not sure. Late."

"We must have gone to bed. Come along after the game. Phil has made huge amounts of chili."

Bramble was delighted. "I don't want to go to the Morris Inn, not after what happened there two weeks ago."

"You will be safe with us. And bring your friends."

"Friends?"

Roger had noticed the couple seated with Bramble. "The Walkers. We all have so much in common."

"Maybe I will," Bramble said, reluctantly.

"If you don't, we won't ever open the door again."

"Aha! So you did hear me last night."

Detective Waring came into view, coming slowly upward, his eyes searching as he climbed. On a hunch, Roger stood and when Waring saw him he looked less anx-

ious. When he reached their row, he took
Roger away for a chat beneath the press
box.

When Roger returned, Bramble was saying to Phil, "I told you those odds were all
wrong."

"They are ahead by two touchdowns."

"Two flukes and nothing since. The second half will tell the story."

But the story it told was not the one
Bramble predicted. On its first drive, Notre
Dame got into the opponent's territory, but
had to settle for a field goal. The opponent
fumbled on the next series, but recovered
on their own ten-yard line. A pass was then
intercepted, and Notre Dame began a series that seemed to go in reverse. In a surprise decision, a field goal was called on
the third down, perhaps out of fear that another play would put them out of reach. The
score was 14-6. And there it stood until
there were only five minutes to go in the
game. But the ball was in the opponent's
hands. Three precious minutes were consumed by running plays. It was clear that
the opponent was playing the clock in the
belief that its margin would stand up. Finally, they had to punt from their own 47,

and although the ball appeared to have been downed by a Southern Cal player on the two-yard line, it was declared to be a touchback. Notre Dame ball on their own 20, with a minute and a half to play.

"What did Waring want?" Phil asked, as if desperate to relieve the tension of the game.

"Things look worse for Hadley."

"How could they?"

"Later."

The first play would figure in replays forever. The quarterback handed off, the back in turn handed off, and then, a real circus play, the ball was pitched back to the quarterback, who after all the razzle-dazzle stood in splendid isolation on his own ten. The pass he threw seemed to have been shot rather than thrown. The split end had proceeded in a leisurely fashion down the field, while the defense was immobilized by the complicated play, but now he turned on the afterburners, running so fast he all but outran the ball. Then he turned and gathered it in and crossed the goal line. 14-12. There was no hesitation. Notre Dame had to go for a two-point conversion. The quarterback called his own number after spreading his line nearly the width of the field. There were two defenders on his back as he went over the line. Pandemonium. The final score was 14-14.

31

There is nothing like a tie to elicit philosophical observations from the fan. He has been granted neither the elation of victory nor the misery of defeat. Disappointment, even recrimination, may be expressed, but these soon fade away. "Neither side deserved to lose," it will be said. "The teams were perfectly matched." And, "It would have been a crime if we (they) had won." This equanimity is not characteristic of a sports fan and, having given it expression, he tends to put the game behind and go on to other things.

So it was that Roger rode back to the

Hesburgh Center with Mrs. Walker on the seat beside him and Phil and their guests following behind. The Walkers had sought to excuse themselves from what they were sure was a party of close friends.

"Close friends," Bramble protested. "These two bums? Come on along and add some tone to the party."

Mr. Walker was more than willing, but Mrs. held back until Phil took her arm, put it through his, and escorted her out to the golf cart. "Your chariot, madam."

" 'The barge she sat in, like a burnished throne,' " intoned Roger, and Mrs. Walker smiled indulgently. Clearly she saw Roger as something of a comic character.

Doubtless she was confirmed in this judgment when they arrived at the apartment, and Roger, in an effort to make everyone feel at home, scooted around the apartment on his wheeled chair, fetching drinks and snacks, adjusting the television so that a West Coast game could be seen if not heard.

"Your pleasure, madam?" he asked Carey Walker.

"What do you have?"

"Whatever you wish."

"I suppose it would be silly to ask for a Brandy Alexander."

"Not at all." Roger laughed. "Remember the adage. It is better to have loved a short woman and lost than never to have loved a tall." Bramble liked that, but Mrs. Walker did not. Too late, Roger remembered the relative heights of the Walkers. Carey could rest her chin on Jim's head. He escaped to the kitchen to prepare her drink. He would have guessed her order would be a French 75.

Phil was a more adept host and within minutes the atmosphere was cordial, even convivial. Bramble and Phil got down to some serious second-guessing of the Notre Dame game plan. Mrs. Walker professed to be astonished at what a wonderful drink Roger had prepared for her. He had just presented her with her third when Greg Whelan arrived. His expression told Roger that the errands the archivist had been on during the game had not been in vain.

"Oh, I know Mr. Whelan," Carey Walker said when Roger introduced the archivist.

"You look as if you have learned something of interest to all of us, Greg."

"I played a copy of the voice message

on Henry Hadley's Decio phone for Mrs. Taylor."

"The housekeeper at the Bourke house," Phil explained to Marcus Bramble.

"You mean Madeline Rune's hysterical message?" Roger coaxed.

"It wasn't Madeline Rune's voice."

"What?" Roger rolled forward in excitement.

"Mrs. Taylor said she would swear on a stack of bibles that wasn't Madeline."

Roger rolled backward. "I must say that I am really not surprised."

"You're not?" Mrs. Walker smiled at him as the teacher smiles at the dullard.

"No. It ties in with those e-mail messages you drew Detective Waring's attention to."

"I don't follow you."

"All those e-mail messages were authentic, of course. I mean, they had been sent to Madeline Rune by Henry Hadley."

"Of course they had."

"It was the last message that was bogus."

Mrs. Walker looked around to see if someone would explain this nonsense.

"It wasn't an e-mail message at all. Simply typed on Madeline's computer, printed out and included with the e-mail messages. Of course, that seemed to make the whole batch look sinister."

Marcus Bramble shook his head. "I'm not following this."

"There is nothing to follow," Carey Walker snorted.

"Marcus, it is quite simple. Someone went to some lengths to incriminate Henry Hadley."

"But I thought he was guilty."

"So did the police. But these new developments change everything." Roger leaned over the arm of his chair toward Mrs. Walker. "These were grievous mistakes. But the bat, Mrs. Walker, that was your undoing."

"What on earth do you mean?"

"Laboratory tests prove that it was the weapon used to kill both of the Runes."

"Of course it was. That is why Henry Hadley has been charged."

"But no fingerprints of his showed up on the bat. Whose fingerprints do you suppose were found?"

There was a frozen moment, then her

eyes flickered to her husband. Obviously, the remark has struck home. She rose slowly to her feet.

"Come, Jim. I think we should leave."

He rose, finishing his drink as he did. Waring arrived as if on cue.

"Here you are," he said cheerily to the Walkers. "Why don't we go downtown and have a nice talk?"

"Let me by," Mrs. Walker said and threw a shoulder into Waring. But Edna Pulchrasky filled the doorway and there was no way anyone was going to get past her.

"I gather you told her," Waring said to Roger.

Roger asked for a conference and whispered for a moment to Waring, who nodded and then went off with the Walkers and Officer Pulchrasky.

"What's he want to talk to them about?" Bramble asked, clearly confused by the past several minutes.

"She killed Madeline and Stanley," Roger said. "Would you care for another drink."

"I need another one," Bramble cried. "Those two claimed that I made promises to them after a long evening in the country

club bar. They said I had signed an agreement to set them up in the Bourke house
and locate my Rockne memorial there." He
called after Phil. "Make that a light one."

"When did you learn that her fingerprints
were on the bat?" Whelan asked.

"Did I say that?"

"Sure you did. That's when she lost it."

"Philip," Roger called. "Did I say that
Mrs. Walker's fingerprints were on the
baseball bat?"

Silence from the kitchen.

"If there were a transcript," Roger said,
"we could review it and you would find that
I asserted no such thing. Not that I think
such fingerprints will be necessary to get a
conviction."

32

Late in January, during a halftime interview at the Super Bowl, in which his team held a seven-point lead, Marcus Bramble turned the discussion to his favorite project, a fitting memorial to Knute Rockne at his alma mater.

"The design has been approved, bids have been let, work on enlarging and reinforcing the island has begun."

There was a model of the neoclassical design in the Knights' apartment, and their eyes went to it as they listened to their new-found friend. Phil said he was getting used to it and Roger claimed to have liked it from the first. Rockne would lie in state in a manner rivaling Napoleon's in Les Invalides, the study of F. X. Bourke would be replicated in the museum and become one of the principal reading rooms. Greg Walsh had been appointed director of the Marcus Bramble Knute Rockne Museum and would be on the building site as work progressed, and later he would oversee the boxing and shipping of the papers from the Bourke house. The study would become an empty shell, but Manfred Dosch put the house on the market, to ensure that his legal fee would be forthcoming. He showed no more confidence than anyone else that the Walkers would be acquitted. The best he could hope for was leniency.

"On what basis?"

"They have lost their only relatives."

"Don't laugh, Roger. It might work."

The Walkers' Florida condo had been occupied by tenants during the time they claimed to have spent there. They had been staying at the Holiday Inn in Michigan City, but of course they could not keep their room during a home game weekend. That Holiday Inn was as sold out as the Morris Inn on game days. That was when the Lansings had removed themselves to Stanley Rune's room at the Evergreen. By that time they had enlisted him in their campaign to turn the Bourke house into a shrine with themselves in residence. Stanley, to his discredit, had colluded with them in a plan that would force Madeline from the house, and even rented a car for them in his name. The night clerk at the Evergreen was now reading *The Professor's House*, but he tore himself away from it long enough to identify Jim Walker as the man who had asked him for a key to the room. He had lost the one he had taken with him on the errand Carey sent him on, losing it where he pushed Stanley's body into the river.

"That little guy?" Phil remarked. "Can you believe it?"

"Marriage to Carey must have toughened him. Or he was afraid not to do what he was told."

"How did he get hold of the Louisville Slugger?"

Miss Imogene sheepishly recalled letting the man into the house when he had come calling. He had asked to be able to leave a note for Henry and had gone downstairs alone. Had she seen him leave?

"He called good-bye as he was going out the door."

Henry Hadley's novel had been rejected, but a well-documented piece of his on the affinity of Batman and Faust had been published in the *PMLA*. Katherine George decided that Henry needed her now and the two had become reconciled.

Menucci had sent Pamela on an extended trip to the old country, where her theatrics would seem prosaic.

"But the cleaning ladies saw her at the Evergreen that Saturday."

"Now they don't think it was Pamela."

Roger may have been the last one to pursue research in the original F. X. Bourke study. It was there that he discovered a box of handwritten materials that required only a glance for him to hurry off to Holy Cross House for a consultation with Father Sebastian Quirk. The priest pushed back the bill of his cap as if to get a better look at the handwritten sheets.

"This is it," he said without hesitation. "How long has it been since I held these? Seventy-some years. But that's Rock's handwriting. No doubt about it. Of course you can check it against other samples and see that I'm right."

He was right, of course, but that was only the beginning of the story. In comparing the manuscript with the published book, Roger discovered two things. First, they did not match, and second, the manuscript was far more accomplished than the printed version of the novel. Comparing key pages where the manuscript moved with verve and style and the corresponding printed pages were stilted and dull raised an interesting problem. How could a draft be better than the finished product?

"You said F. X. Bourke helped Rockne with the novel?"

"I would turn over the manuscript and get back typescript."

The typescript had been produced on the old typewriter that stood next to F. X. Bourke's desk.

"What did Rockne think of Bourke's help?"

"He was grateful as could be."

"I wonder if he ever read the edited version?"

Of course Quirk had no way of knowing that. Roger did not pass on to the old priest his own suspicion. Clearly Bourke had taken a reasonably well told story and turned it into an amateur effort. The only passages he did not touch were those in which Rockne described a game in progress. To have altered these might have produced discrepancies with Rockne's book on coaching and others might have learned of Bourke's role in the writing of Knute Rockne's only novel.

"Which of them wrote the dedication?"

"To Arnold J. McInerny? Oh, that was Rock. Bourke said he wouldn't touch a word of it."

Had Bourke meant to leave a clue to be discovered posthumously? No one who could write that dedication could have written so bad a novel. But at the time Bourke had guarded against competition from his old friend. Rockne had been a better player than Bourke, he had become the premier coach in the nation, and Bourke had not wanted to be eclipsed in his chosen territory by Rockne. The manuscript was not a great novel, but it was close to the standard set in Bourke's McNaughton novels. Indeed, it clearly owed much to them. By altering it as he had, Bourke ensured that

The Four Winners would be considered a rare lapse into ineptitude on the part of the great coach.

On the screen, Marcus Bramble was telling an astonished interviewer that Knute Rockne had written a novel.

"I never knew that. What's it like?"

Bramble, practiced in such matters, turned to face the camera, holding a copy of the book.

"I think this is one of the greatest novels ever written."